CH00498645

Grinch Reaper

SLEEPER SEALs SERIES BOOK #8

Also Connected to the
Dangerous Curves Series

Donna Michaels

*New York Times & USA Today
Bestselling Author*

GRINCH REAPER
Sleeper SEALs Series/Book 8

Copyright © 2017 Donna Michaels
Cover Art by CoverMe Photography © 2017

All rights reserved. No part of this book may be used, stored, reproduced or transmitted in any form without written permission from the publisher, except for a brief quotation in a book review.

This is a work of fiction. Names, characters, places, and incidents are products of the author's imagination or used fictitiously. Any resemblance to actual events or locales or persons living or dead is entirely coincidental.

This book contains material protected under International and Federal Copyright Laws and Treaties. Any unauthorized reprint or use of this material is prohibited. No part of this book may be reproduced in any form or by any means, electronic or mechanical, including photocopying, or recording, or by any information storage and retrieval system without express written permission from the author.

ISBN-13: 978-1981970957
ISBN-10: 1981970959

Print edition December 2017
Book 8 in Sleeper SEALs Series

Grinch Reaper

SLEEPER SEALs SERIES BOOK #8

Connected to the Dangerous Curves Series

Donna Michaels

A NOTE TO THE READER

Thank you for purchasing GRICH REAPER! This is the 8th book in the Sleeper SEALs Series, and I'm so honored and excited to be included alongside eleven talented authors writing in this world.

The characters in this story were so much fun to write! I know this series is about the Sleeper SEALs, but my heroine was a force of nature and such a joy to write. I admittedly, had to reign her in at times. This book is connected to my romantic military suspense series, Dangerous Curves, so you can bet you'll see more of Bella and Matteo in future DC books. They're too much fun to let rest with their HEA.

If you enjoy GRINCH REAPER, you'll love the rest of the agents in my Dangerous Curves Series. But don't worry, each are written as stand alones, so they can be read in any order.

Thanks for reading,

~Donna
www.donnamichaelsauthor.com

A NOTE FROM THE AUTHOR

Enjoy other military suspense books from
Donna Michaels

~*Dangerous Curves Series*~
Knight's SEAL –KW (#1)
Locke and Load (#2)
A DAYE with a SEAL–KW (#3)
Cowboy LAWE (#4)

Visit DonnaMichaelsAuthor.com for more titles and release dates, and to sign up for her Newsletter. Enjoy exclusive reads, enter subscriber only contests, and be the first to know about upcoming books!

Prologue

*If you haven't read the Universal Prologue, which is exactly the same in all the Sleeper SEAL books, you can find it here:
https://sleeperseals.com/about-the-series/

Isabella "Banshee" Monroe straightened the short jacket of her flight attendant disguise before carrying a tray of neurotoxin infused coffees to the three passengers on the private jet bound for Islamabad. Dialing her features to relaxed, she embraced the cold, unfeeling, calm required to carry out her mission.

Kill the men who financed Samir Al-Jamil, the mastermind behind recent school bombings in Iraq.

A coordinated ground attack was underway for that bastard and was not her concern. She was sanctioned to take out the Pakistani businessmen with ties to ISIS. They would no longer help front the movement. Today, she was terminating their business dealings.

Terminating them.

She lived for this type of op. Her specialty. Her wheelhouse.

Recruited over two years ago from the Marines to work for a government-sanctioned special ops unit through the CIA, Bella was the only female on a six-person team. Some missions required all-hands-on-deck, others, like today, were solo.

Her favorite kind.

"Here you are." Handing out the drinks, she hid a smile as their conversation halted. A waste of time. She understood Pashto, and already knew about their plans to meet with a leader in Islamabad to turn over the three briefcases full of cash attached to their wrists. "Is there anything else I can get for you, gentlemen?"

One ignored her. Another shook his head, while the third reached out to glide his hand up her leg that was bared below the short skirt of her uniform. No doubt, this was the reason he'd hired a flight attendant for this trip.

"Yes, I'll have you," Heydar Rostami replied, his gaze as dark as his soul. Soon, his expression would not be so smug.

"Now, Mr. Rostami, you know I'm not on the menu. But," she leaned close and winked, "for two thousand American, I could be."

Smirking, he released her leg to fish a wallet from inside his suit coat, removed a wad of cash, and handed it to her. "Done."

"Well, all right then." She returned his grin and shoved the money in her bra. Playing with the jerks kept them off balance. "Just let me deliver the pilot his coffee, and I'll be back to fill your...special order."

Satisfaction increased the leer in his gaze as he sat back and remarked in his native tongue about the three of them introducing her to the mile-high club before he reclaimed his money. He didn't know she understood every word, nor did he realize his words brought back memories of her childhood crush.

The mile-high club...

Once upon a time, when she was a teenager and naïve, Bella used to fantasize about her best friend's older brother taking her in a plane...literally. A ripple of longing fluttered through her belly. Dammit. She hadn't seen the handsome Italian in years, and he was still messing with her head.

And she was in the middle of a freaking job.

With a steady indrawn then exhaled breath, she buried the unwanted thoughts and refocused on her mission.

The guy sitting across from Heydar lifted his cup in a mock toast, and their laughter echoed through the cabin before they sipped their coffees.

That's it, drink up, fellas, she silently urged, adrenaline rushing through her veins. They were making it all too easy.

A scowl rippled across the third man's face as he glared at her through eyes so full of hate they appeared black. An extremist. Like the terrorist who killed her father. The reason she was a terrorist hunter. Bella took solace in the knowledge that someday, Rasheed Al-Zahawi's dossier would come into her unit's crosshair. Until then, she rid the world of the bastards one by one.

The need to remove the knife from her garter and shove it into this particular bastard's stone-cold heart, shook through Bella's fingers. But he deserved worse. Deserved the fate he already set into motion by drinking half his laced coffee.

It was already too late for the three men. By the time she returned from the cockpit, the neurotoxin would've taken effect and prepared the terrorists for interrogation before their demise.

Three down, one to go.

Back in the small beverage nook, Bella poured coffee into a cup, added poison instead of neurotoxin, then headed for the cockpit. She didn't need the pilot alive.

Once inside, she closed the door and addressed the Iranian the others called Behram. "Mr. Rostami wants to know where we are."

Behram rattled off coordinates putting them over the middle of the Indian Ocean. Perfect. Exactly where she needed to be.

She smiled and handed him the coffee. "Thank you."

After flipping on the auto pilot, he took a sip. A second later, he dropped the cup, his gaze shooting to hers, fear and anger glittering in his eyes as he reached for the gun holstered under his jacket. Too late. Behram's mouth started to foam, and in a heartbeat, his body slackened, and his breathing stopped.

He got off lucky.

Killing innocent women and children at school was the lowest of the low.

A modicum of warmth rippled through her cold heart as she slipped into the empty co-pilot seat and punched several buttons to change course, speed, and latitude to take them toward a carrier located eighty-nine miles northwest of their location.

Her rendezvous point wasn't far.

Neither was justice for those who perished in the Mosul school bombings. She would ensure these men never financed another attack that took innocent lives.

5

Opening a small compartment to her right, Bella quickly calculated their arrival time and removed the satellite phone she'd stashed before the flight. "Operation Bird Bath on schedule," she said, after contacting her commander. "Repeat. Operation Bird Bath on schedule. Meet at rendezvous."

"Roger."

The one-word response was an affirmation to proceed.

It meant no bogies in the vicinity, which gave her approximately eleven minutes to extract information. She hung up and opened the cockpit door a sliver. Enough time had elapsed for the neurotoxins to kick in and secure a captive audience.

A quick peek confirmed their inability to fight. Each man sat frozen, one angled unnaturally as if he'd tried to get up, another leaned forward slightly, with his cup halted in midair, and the scowling one sat immobile, one large hand crossed over his mid-section as if reaching for his holstered gun.

"Sorry, gentlemen." As she neared, she dug the money out of her bra and tossed the cash on the table between them. "The kitchen's closed."

"What have you done to us?" Heydar's tone was strained, like the other two men who were cursing her in Pashto.

The fun was just beginning.

With her pulse kicking up a few notches, she removed their guns and set them on a seat across the aisle. "Like that?" Turning to face them, she smiled. "I dosed you with a paralyzing agent, mixed with truth serum. It's something a chemist friend of mine cooked up. But don't worry. It'll wear off in an hour."

Of course, by then, they'd be at the bottom of the ocean.

"I'm gonna fuckin' kill you," *scowler* man growled out, in English this time.

An image of the broken and bloodied bodies of children—half buried under the rubble of their demolished school—flashed through her mind. Even though she knew better, Bella leaned close enough for her breath to hit the monster's face as she used his words against him. "I'd like to see you fuckin' try."

With a half curse/half cry, he spit at her. The very reason she shouldn't have gotten close. Rookie mistake. And Bella was no rookie, despite the fact she allowed emotions to cloud her judgment. She jerked back, but it was unnecessary because his jaw was too stiff for good aim. It hit the empty seat across from him.

She straightened up and smirked. "You can't even do that right."

The vein in his temple and the one at the bottom of his neck pulsed to near bursting. He started ranting about her death and Allah, but

Bella tuned him out as she headed back to the beverage station to retrieve a few more things she'd stashed before takeoff. A waterproof duffle bag, the backpack she never left home without, jumpsuit, headgear, and sneakers.

"Behram," the man across from Heydar hollered toward the cockpit.

She shook her head. "Don't bother. He can't help you."

"You paralyzed him, too?" His raised tone echoed through the cabin. "How is he flying the plane?"

"No. I didn't paralyze him," she replied, noting a flash of relief flicker through his eyes. That wouldn't do. "I laced his coffee with cyanide."

Horror filled his gaze.

Much better.

"You killed him?"

She smiled and rolled her eyes. "Of course. But I waited until he engaged the auto pilot first."

Technically, she had her own license and could easily fly the plane. Unfortunately for them though, it wasn't part of her mission.

"What do you want from us?" Heydar spoke up again, eyes cold, face red.

Finally. Someone asking the right questions.

The fun she was having at their expense was probably a sin, anyway. But, considering the countless lives the terrorists they financed took each year, she figured her soul could handle another black mark.

"Simple." Leaving her jump gear on the floor by the beverage station, she met his gaze and approached to set her pack on the table across the aisle from him. "I'd love for you to tell me what Samir was planning to do with the money in these briefcases."

One by one, she cut the chains that secured the cases to their wrists, using the all-in-one tool she'd removed from her pack. Not a peep, an oath, or a sound was uttered. Unease trickled down Bella's spine in a pinpricking sensation. She had a feeling the answer was bigger than the school bombings.

After shoving the cases into a watertight compartment in the duffle bag, she twisted around to stare at the suddenly silent men. "Come on, guys. Nothing? Time to put that truth serum to work. What was the money for?"

There was a lot of it. The cases were heavy. Apprehension joined the unease and pricked her shoulders. Whatever Samir had planned, it was big.

"Don't know," Heydar finally replied, in a tone too strained to be truthful.

Bullshit.

Forcing her breathing to remain even, she held her frustration in check and concentrated on digging the cell phones from their pockets, and the laptop from Heydar's bag. With luck, the tech team would discover useful information on the devices, which, in turn, would point her in the direction to hunt more terrorists.

A quick glance at the clock on one of the phones she shoved into her backpack, along with the laptop, informed her there were seven minutes left until rendezvous. No time to waste.

After retrieving her satellite phone from the cockpit and adding to her backpack, she activated a tracking device in the duffle bag, before closing the bag and securing it with a zip tie. Since the money and devices were taken care of, it was interrogation time.

Embracing her job, Bella stepped to Heydar and bent to stare right in his face, noting dilated eyes and beads of sweat gathered across his brow. "Stop fighting the serum, sweetheart. It won't hurt so much. Come on. Tell me, what is Samir planning?"

"Go to hell," *scowler* man answered for him.

In Pashto, again.

She could use that.

Narrowing her eyes, she pretended not to understand. "What? Speak English. What is he planning?"

Heydar laughed. "Samir will make sure America has a reason not to forget your holidays," he taunted, also in Pashto.

That's it, boys. Tell me everything.

To continue with the charade, Bella clenched her jaw and slammed a fist onto the table in front of him. "English! Dammit! What is he doing? Who is he paying?"

All three men laughed and jeered as they spewed details in their native tongue, having way too much fun taunting her.

Giving her everything she wanted.

Idiots. It was surreal. Or perhaps it was the hand of fate giving her a break for a change.

Whatever the reason for the easy info extraction, she stored everything they told her in her head without blinking, even when they mentioned her hometown. But when the man across from Heydar said the name of the terrorist burned in her brain for over thirteen years, everything inside Bella froze. Except her heart. It rocked hard in her chest.

When she was certain they had nothing left to tell, she ripped the satellite phone from her pack, and holding the men's gazes, contacted her boss. "Take Samir alive. Target is Atlantic City during the holidays. Two sympathizers already in place, prepping for Rasheed Al-Zahawi's arrival. Repeat. Rasheed Al-Zahawi. They don't know the venue, or the names of the sympathizers."

If she wasn't in shock from hearing the name of the man who'd murdered her father,

11

she probably would've laughed at the shock trying to widen the prisoners' eyes and slacken their jaws in their frozen state.

"Roger," her commander said in a clipped tone. "Rendezvous in five. Out."

"Roger. Out."

Shit just got real.

Her fingers shook as she shoved the phone in her pack, and wondered briefly if the team on the ground had already taken out Samir. With luck, she'd gotten word to them in time. The monster could still prove useful to take down a bigger monster.

Today was the day.

Homeland, the CIA, all the letter agencies had waited over a decade for this scum to stick his head out of a cave so they could bring justice down on his sorry ass. As a hunter, Bella had waited over two years. As a Marine, she'd waited almost a decade.

But as a daughter? Oh…as a daughter, she had waited thirteen long years for the bastard to pay for killing her father.

"You speak Pashto?" Heydar's tense voice drifted to her as she retrieved two parachutes from a compartment behind the cockpit and secured one to the duffle bag full of their money.

"Yes. And three other languages." She kicked off her shoes, slipped a jumpsuit on over her uniform, then shoved her feet into her sneakers.

Heydar muttered an oath.

A smile tugged her lips. His aha moment. *Sucks to be him.*

Donning her backpack in front and the other chute on her back, Bella snickered. "I know. I'm a bit of a slacker. Still, you'd be surprised what you pick up when you hunt terrorists." Winking, she grabbed her headgear and the duffle/chute combo from the floor and headed toward the emergency lever.

"Wait! What are you doing?"

She turned to face them and shrugged. "I'm getting off this bird. It's going to crash, and you're all going to die. There's no pilot, remember?"

Okay, it was probably childish to taunt them back, but…damn, it felt good.

"But what about the autopilot?" the man across from Heydar asked, swallowing audibly while his gaze darted to the closed cockpit door.

She snorted. "Dude, autopilot flies, not lands. But it doesn't matter. I programmed the plane to fly right into the ocean—after I leave, of course. So, I guess, technically, it is going to land," she said, digging one of their phones from her pack to glance at the time. "In about four minutes."

Her rendezvous on the carrier was now in two.

"Who are you?" Heydar asked, sweat now running down his face.

Shoulders back, she stood at attention. "Staff Sergeant Isabella Monroe, United States Marine Corps, but most terrorists know me as Banshee."

Right before they died.

Adrenaline coursed through her body, heating the blood in her veins. Time to finish her mission. She grasped the duffle bag tight, then opened the door. The cabin immediately depressurized, and the plane tilted, causing the men to jerk out of their seats.

Holding onto the door frame, she glanced back at the screaming men. "This is for the Mosul women and children. Enjoy the rest of your flight. It's gonna be a short one. Hoorah!"

With a salute, she jumped out, already eager to start her next mission. It had to be Rasheed. Just the fact his name was spoken, no doubt, already started chatter amongst the agencies. She yanked the ripcord on the duffle bag, releasing the chute two seconds before activating her own.

At the end of the day, though, Bella didn't care who made Rasheed pay, just as long as he did. Obviously, she prayed her agency was green lit to take out the sorry excuse for a human. Her commander already knew if the file fell into his hands, there was no way he was keeping her off the mission. In fact, he'd already told her she was his first choice.

Unlike the police force and other agencies that didn't allow an agent to work a case if they were personally involved, her agency embraced it. There wasn't a weapon more powerful to bring down a terrorist than a personally motivated agent.

The ruthless hunting the ruthless.

Truer words.

If she was given the mission, nothing and no one would stop Bella from taking down Rasheed.

Chapter One

"Two small cokes, and a large supreme, hold the anchovies."

Making pizza wasn't exactly using Matteo "Reaper" Santarelli's skillset. Holding back a grimace, he started on the pie while one of his employees handled the money and drinks for the young couple who ordered on the other side of the L-shaped glass counter in front of Santarelli's Pizza.

A former Navy SEAL, he was a highly trained special operative tossing dough in a small boardwalk pizza shop in Atlantic City, instead of grenades on a mission on foreign soil with his brothers. It wasn't right, and it ate at him every minute of the twenty-eight days, seven hours, thirty-five minutes, and twelve seconds since he left the teams. Forced out because of an injury was one thing, but to walk away from his brothers when he was still able and capable was another. It caused a burning knot— the size of the ball of dough he flattened on the flour covered counter—to twist his gut tight.

"Hi, Matteo." A gust of cold December air followed his father's old friend and business neighbor, Omar Gupta, inside.

Like many of the boardwalk shop owners, the middle-aged man was an immigrant. He came to the U.S. from India with his family when he was fourteen, and took over the corner sundry shop next door after his father passed two decades ago.

"Hey, Omar." Nodding, Matteo tossed the stretched dough high, using his pizzaiolo skills from his many years working in his family's three shops up and down the Jersey coast. Some things you never forget. Catching the dough with his fingertips, he immediately sent it spinning again without letting it rest. "The usual?"

"Yes, thank you." Omar closed the door in the fogged-up glass partition separating the shop from the cold wind whipping down the boardwalk.

During the warmer months, the partition was open, allowing people to walk right up to the counter from outside. It also allowed heat from the ovens behind Matteo to escape, although during the summer, it mixed with the hot, humid ocean air, creating an almost unbearable workspace. Air conditioning wasn't an option. Not with the front wide open in the warm seasons. Ceiling fans and two huge oscillating ones in the dining area behind their workspace kept it tolerable.

Little had Matteo known, working in the suffocating heat growing up had conditioned him for missions overseas.

God, he missed them.

Missed the action. Helping others. The sense of purpose...his brothers.

Clenching his jaw, he set the flattened dough on a tray then slapped another ball of dough onto the floured counter and pounded it with his fist.

"How is your father?" Omar asked, yanking him out of his well of frustration and guilt.

He blew out a breath, and in an instant, all the tension digging at his shoulders and spine dissipated. Instead of having their six, he now had his dad's.

A month ago, Angelo Santarelli suffered a stroke in the very spot Matteo now stood. He'd been working alone, and was damn lucky to survive. At fifty-five, he was also way too young and stubborn to remain partially paralyzed.

"He's okay." With the help of physical therapy, he was already starting to show some movement. "You know my dad, he's obstinate." After adding toppings to the pie, Matteo shoved it into the oven, before making Omar's spicy turkey wrap. "Pretty soon, he'll be steady enough on his feet and walking with a walker."

Omar nodded, a slight tug to his lips. "Stubborn is his middle name. What about speaking? How is that going?"

He sighed, and an invisible weight settled heavily on Matteo's shoulders. "Still garbled and slurred."

Like his writing.

Early on, Matteo got the impression his dad was trying to tell him something. Each day he visited the rehab center, he slid a pencil in his father's curled fingers, but so far, his dad only managed to scribble. It frustrated the man. Matteo could tell by the clenched jaw and the way he snapped the pencil in half.

Some of that anger and frustration bit at Matteo's spine as he set the turkey wrap on the counter with a thud. He'd never felt so damn helpless in his life.

He couldn't help his brothers. Couldn't help his father.

Omar reached for the plate, warmth and understanding softening his expression. "You are a good son to give up your career to take care of your father."

There wasn't anyone else. A few years ago, Matteo's mother died from a heart attack, and his sister Nina lived an hour away in Cape May with her husband Joe, two-year-old daughter, and infant son. He never gave it a second thought.

"My dad needed me." He shrugged. End of story.

It just sucked he had to give up one family to take care of the other.

That didn't mean he completely ruled out returning to his unit, though. Thanks to physical therapy and a can-do attitude, his father's prognosis was good. It might take some time, but he felt confident his father would eventually lead a fairly normal life.

Thank God.

But even if he didn't return to the teams, there was no way he'd take over supervising the shops for the rest of his life. It didn't spark adrenaline, or fulfill his need to help people. Joe managed their Wildwood location, and was more than capable of taking over the supervision of all the shops if needed. The only reason Matteo hadn't suggested it in the first place was because something about his father's situation niggled at the back of his mind. He wasn't entirely convinced his father's stroke had been brought on by natural causes.

There was a head injury, too. No one was certain if it happened during his father's fall, or was the reason behind it. When questioned, the doctors couldn't give a definite answer. So,

Matteo left the teams, moved into his dad's shore house, took over the shops, and was waiting for his father to recover enough to communicate with him.

And just in case his suspicions were correct, he wanted to work the Atlantic City location. Walk in his father's shoes. Study the clientele. Get a feel for the place. But most of the people who came in were neighboring shop owners, some Matteo had known his whole life. And the one's he didn't know never raised any red flags.

Maybe he was just jaded, having witnessed the dark side of human nature for too long. Perhaps he was reading things wrong. Projecting his mistrust. It was possible his dad really had suffered a stroke and hit his head when he collapsed to the floor. An accident.

God, he hoped so, because otherwise...his father's attacker might've been someone he knew.

If there was even the slightest chance that was true, Matteo had no choice but to suspect everyone. And he did. For weeks now, he studied each person who walked in the door, noting their demeanor, what they wore, ordered, who they spoke to, where they sat. Nothing, and no one, was above suspicion. Even Omar.

"Tell your father I was asking about him," the man said, taking his usual table up front. "I tried to visit, but only family was allowed."

He regarded Omar, noting a slight tightening to his lips and eyes. Was concern for his father the cause? Or concern for himself?

Matteo's gut knotted tight. Christ, this fucking sucked.

"I'll tell him." He nodded, wishing it was all a bad dream. That his father never suffered a stroke, and he was still a SEAL with his buddies in some God-forsaken country on a mission he couldn't talk about. Not home, scrutinizing every damn person who walked through the fucking door.

Lack of adrenaline was making him paranoid. Nuts. He was bored. Used to operating at three hundred miles an hour. He wasn't cut out for normal speed. He needed a mission. Something other than stretching dough.

Back in his teens, he enjoyed showing off those skills, talking to customers, smiling at the girls, watching his sister and her best friend laugh as they sat at the corner table in the back. Shifting his gaze to the now empty table, he visualized the two girls there, plain as day. Eyes twinkling, heads thrown back laughing, gaining the attention of every teenage boy in a two-mile vicinity.

Warmth spread through Matteo, easing the tightness from his chest. There was something about Bella Monroe that had always made him smile. The daughter of his father's Gulf War buddy, she was from New York City, but spent summers here at her grandmother's, until her father died and mother moved them here permanently.

Her vivacious personality could fill an empty room. Even now, his lips twitched at the memory of the girl whose smile used to rule the beat of his heart. A cute daredevil he watched mature into a spirited beauty, with long brown hair and gorgeous green eyes that always warmed at the sight of him.

His dad—also Bella's godfather—had given him the task to watch over her like a sister. But once she hit her teens, Matteo realized he had no brotherly feelings for her whatsoever. They were strong. Protective. *Passionate.* Not brotherly.

Keeping the horny teenage boys from her hadn't been a problem, he'd been more than happy to warn them off—because he'd been one of them. The fact she reciprocated his feelings only made things harder. Literally. Cold shower became Matteo's middle name. For years, he resisted her without incident, until the night of her graduation. Oh, he still resisted, but he broke her heart in the process, then flew to Illinois the next day to start Naval Special

Warfare Prep school. They'd only crossed paths once since then, at his mother's funeral, five years ago.

"Have you seen Bella yet?" Omar asked, as if reading his mind.

He smiled, pulse kicking up at the possibility of seeing her again. "No. Not yet." He'd heard she'd moved back into her late grandmother's house a few years ago, but so far, every time he glanced out his father's kitchen window he saw no signs of her next door.

Omar swiped his mouth with a napkin and nodded. "I thought I spotted her at the airport about an hour ago. It's hard to keep track. She's always flying off to do work for that travel magazine."

He frowned. "Airport?"

Why was Omar at the airport?

"Yeah, I was picking up my son and thought I spotted her," Omar informed between bites. "She deals blackjack part time at the Capris, too, so I'm sure you'll run into her soon."

A smile tugged his lips. Bella never could sit idle.

And he'd read about the newest casino when he first got home. With major backers from the west coast, the Capris was built at the north end of the boardwalk. It was nice to see the large resort brought in major headliners, concerts, conventions, and sporting events that gave a much-needed boost to the city's economy. It boggled Matteo's mind the number of casinos that came and went since he left home.

"I should get back to work. When you see your dad, tell him I was asking about him," Omar said, tossing his garbage in the trash on his way to the door.

Matteo nodded. "Will do."

The first few days, after his dad had been transferred from the hospital to the rehab center, Matteo had stayed for hours, but his father appeared agitated, grunting and fussing. Then it'd dawned on him that his dad probably wanted him to cover down at the shop. The second he'd made the suggestion, his father settled down, and since Matteo had wanted to investigate anyway, it'd worked out. Now, he visited twice a day, once in the morning and again in the afternoon.

A quick glance at the clock on the wall confirmed the dining room had thinned out because the lunch rush was over. He also noted it was almost time for the two teens on co-op from the local high school to come in for their shift, along with Russell, the afternoon manager, who'd worked at the shop for nearly two decades. Their arrival would free him up to visit his dad.

As he pulled a pie from the oven and set it on the counter to cut, Matteo was wondering what kind of mood his dad would be in today when the door opened and a familiar awareness trickled down his spine.

Without even glancing at the door, he knew it wasn't Russell or the two teens that walked in. No. Only one person sent blood rushing through his veins and his pulse thundering in his ears as if he were running an op.

Bella.

She was the adrenaline fix he craved. Hell, she was a whole lot of things he craved.

Bracing himself for the onslaught of awareness he knew was coming by making eye contact, he glanced at the woman who ruled his heart. A zing instantly ricocheted through his chest and knocked his heart back into place.

Damn, he hadn't realized it was out of place until that moment.

"Matteo…" Dressed in jeans, black boots, and matching leather jacket that looked as soft as the green sweater hugging her ample curves, she had a black backpack slung carelessly over her shoulder and an expression dialed to "I don't care." She was trouble. A major threat to his self-control. If he thought her an unstoppable force before, then the adult Bella was now a damn force of nature.

Her hair was still a warm brown like melted chocolate, and eyes a deep mesmerizing green that could stop waves from crashing into the shore, but the confident tilt of her chin and the lethal grace in her steps awoke something primal deep inside him.

He was in big trouble, because despite the adult changes, she was still the daughter of his father's best friend. Still his father's goddaughter. Still Matteo's surrogate sister.

Still forbidden.

"Hello, Bella." He set the pie cutter down and turned to face her fully, gripping the counter to keep from jumping over and pulling her close.

The shock rounding her eyes disappeared, leaving her gaze dark with concern. "What are *you* doing here?"

He chuckled. "Nice to see you again, too."

"Of course, it's good to see you," she said with a shake of her head. "But why are you here? You're a SEAL. You don't just come home to sling pizza, especially when your duty station is over a five-hour drive away." Her chin tilted. "Unless you flew in from Norfolk."

The fact she knew those distances sent a ripple of surprise through him. Why? Had she thought about him? Thought about visiting him? That ripple turned into an unexpected flood of warmth. Shit. Yeah, he was in trouble.

He opened his mouth to respond, but she narrowed her gaze and searched his face.

"No." She shook her head again. "You didn't fly in. Where's your dad? What happened to him?"

Matteo felt her fear before he watched it drain the color from her face.

"He had a stroke. But he's okay," he rushed to add.

"A stroke?" She reeled back. "Are you kidding me? He's only in his mid-fifties, and not on any blood pressure medication. How could he have a stroke? Did he have an aneurysm?"

An invisible weight lifted from his shoulders. Damn, it was good to hear someone else voice his concern. And yet, he didn't want others to know about his suspicions.

"Let's go in the office," he said, motioning toward the back of the shop. "Joe can watch over things."

His worker nodded as Matteo walked passed to meet her on the other side of the counter. What he had to say was only for her ears. She must've clued in, because she quietly followed him through the brightly lit dining room and through the door leading to the supply room, then through a door on the right that led to the small office.

He'd barely gotten the door closed behind them when she clamped her fingers around his arm and turned him to face her, but she immediately released him. No doubt, because she felt the same crazy-ass current that passed through their connection.

"All right. What the hell is going on, Matteo?" she asked, rubbing her palm on her jeans.

"A few weeks ago, Omar came in for his lunch and found my father on the floor behind the counter." His stomach knotted just thinking about what could've happened if Omar hadn't walked in. "He was rushed to the ER. Luckily, I was on base when my sister called to tell me Dad had suffered a stroke. I took leave and drove up."

She set her backpack on a nearby chair, and her shapely ass against the back of his desk. Lucky desk. "You're not on leave now, are you?"

His heart rocked. Nothing had changed. He didn't even bother to question how the hell she figured that out. Bella always knew him better than he knew himself.

"No," he replied. "Dad's recovery is going to take a while. He has to relearn to walk and talk."

Drawing in a breath, she pushed from the desk, stepped close, and silently slid her arms around him. No platitudes or meaningless words of comfort fell from her lips as her face

29

rested against his shoulder. The woman knew better than most that sometimes things didn't work out okay. He wrapped his arms around her and stood quietly for a moment, enjoying the feel of her hands lightly stroking up and down his back. The simple contact, the comfort meant more to him than anything else she could've said or done.

He knew...somehow, he knew deep inside that her commiseration wasn't just because of his dad. It was for the loss he suffered giving up the teams. Damn, it endeared her to him even more. The invisible wall he'd erected around his heart nearly a decade earlier, cracked, allowing warmth to slide in.

Holding Bella was a bad idea, and yet, Matteo couldn't bring himself to let go. Not yet. Unable to resist, he closed his eyes and buried his face in her hair, enjoying the rare feel of her in his arms. The luxury, the gift, would have to sustain him for the next few years, so he soaked it all in. Her softness, and strength. The way her breathing, her pulse...her heartbeat synced in time with his.

A strand of her silky hair grazed his jaw. The scent—much like the woman—a contradiction of sweetness and spice, made him want to inhale her.

Which would go against his father's wishes.

Mustering up the strength to let her go, he was surprised when Bella pushed out of the embrace first. She cleared her throat and stepped back to lean against the desk again, her gaze friendly, but guarded.

None of those actions were synonymous with the old Bella. She would've held on and tried to kiss him. In fact, the last time they were together that was exactly what had happened. A palpable memory rose in his body of the feel of the soft swell of her breasts brushing his arm through the silky material of the blue dress he knew she wore in honor of his service in the Navy. It'd taken all the strength he'd possessed to avoid her mouth and push her away that night.

An act he was both grateful for, and regretted at the same time.

Like now, he was relieved she'd stepped back, and admittedly a little put out. Had her feelings for him changed?

Jesus, what the hell did it matter? He fought back a grimace. They couldn't have a relationship anyway. And yet…

"So, what exactly aren't you telling me, Matteo?"

His heart rocked in his chest. "What do you mean?" Was he that damn transparent?

She quirked a brow. "You know what I mean. Your dad. What aren't you telling me about his stroke?"

Dad.

Guilt flushed through him, weighing down his shoulders like a hundred-pound rucksack. He thought she'd meant... A quick mental shake cleared his head and got his mind back on track.

"He also suffered a head injury."

The only movement she made was the slight narrowing of her eyes. "When he fell? Or before?"

He blew out a breath. "The doctors aren't sure."

"So...his stroke might not have been an accident," she stated, instead of asked.

A shiver raced down his spine at the cold fury darkening her gaze.

He could relate.

"Yes." He thrust a hand through his hair, and gripped the back of his neck. "And he was working alone, so there were no witnesses either way."

"What about the security footage?" She nodded toward the monitor displaying a live feed of the shop with Joe making a Stromboli out front.

"Nothing," he grumbled. "Apparently, Dad only had the cameras out there for show. I immediately rectified that." It was the first thing he changed when he got to the shop.

She muttered an oath, "I love your dad, but he's the most stubborn man I know. If he causes me to go gray before he does, I swear I'm going to kick his ass."

He bit back a grin. Bella never did mince words. "Stubborn doesn't cover it."

"Sorry, Matteo." She sighed. "I had no idea his cameras were only for show or I would've installed an active system myself."

Although he wondered briefly what a photojournalist/blackjack dealer knew about installing security systems, he waved her off. "Don't worry about it. Like I said, stubborn doesn't cover it."

A smirk tugged her lips and sparked in her eyes. "I seem to recall another stubborn Santarelli."

"Hey...you shouldn't talk about my sister like that," he teased, then smiled as her laughter echoed around them.

"You know perfectly well I meant you, squid." Her gaze continued to sparkle, and it warmed him from head to toe, reminding him of when he'd found shelter after completing a nasty, cold weather op.

The longer he held her gaze, the higher his body temperature rose...and smaller the distance between them appeared. She must've felt the same, because her expression sobered, and the air around them crackled and heated.

Damn. Apparently, their connection had matured, too.

Every damn inch of his body became acutely aware of every sweet curve of hers.

How the hell was he supposed to keep his distance when an invisible energy drew him near? Sucked him close like a vacuum?

Once again, it was Bella who broke the spell. She dropped her gaze and straightened her jacket, and he found it easier to breathe. And think.

"You should get that," she said, nodding toward his crotch.

For a split second, Matteo's mind blanked, until he felt his pocket vibrate with his ringing phone. Dumbass. Swallowing an oath, he whipped out the phone and answered without looking at the caller ID.

"Is this Matteo Santarelli?" a man asked in a clipped tone.

His heart dropped to the floor. Was it the rehab center? He pulled the phone from his ear to glance at the screen, then released a breath and set the phone back to his ear when he noted a D.C. area code. "Yes. And you are?"

"This is retired Navy Commander Greg Lambert. Is this line secured?"

Matteo had never worked with Lambert, but he'd certainly heard of him through one of his old commanders. "You went through BUDs with Commander Knight. And no, sir. This line isn't secure."

Bella's brow rose as if she recognized Knight's name. Which was crazy. Why would a travel magazine photojournalist know a former SEAL Commander recruited by the CIA for their Special Operations Group?

She opened her backpack, removed a satellite phone, and handed it to him.

Which was probably the reason she raised a brow.

"But I can call you back on one," he told Lambert.

"Excellent. I'll be standing by," the commander told him, before the line went dead.

He waved the satellite phone at Bella. "Thanks. I need to call him back. Uh…why do you have this?"

She grinned. "Because I travel to remote places and a cell phone doesn't always cut it."

Ah. He nodded. "True."

He was really striving for dumbass of the year today.

Punching in the number Lambert had used to call him on his cell, Matteo contemplated asking Bella to wait in the dining room so he could talk in private, but he had a weird feeling he needed to keep an eye on her.

Or perhaps it was just a personal need.

"I'll wait for you in the dining room," she said, as if reading his mind. Damn woman always liked to rebel. "All of a sudden, I have a deep craving for you...I mean, one of your pizzas." Grabbing her backpack, she winked before leaving him with both of his heads swelling.

"Santarelli? Hello? Is that you?"

It took him a moment to realize Commander Lambert was speaking to him through the phone he held to his ear. Forget dumbass, he was acting like a fucking idiot.

Because he was one.

"Yes, sir. And the line is secure," he said. "What can I do for you?"

"First of all, how is your father?" Lambert asked, catching him off guard.

Chapter Two

Matteo cocked his head. "Okay. He has a long road ahead, but he's a fighter."

"So are you, from what I've heard."

He reeled back. "Exactly what have you heard, and from whom?"

Lambert chuckled. "Jameson Knight. As you already mentioned, he and I go way back. So when I was tasked to head an initiative to take down terrorist sleeper cells in this country, I put the word out to a few of my peers for recommendations. Knight supplied your name. Even sent me a detailed file. You're a damn good asset to our country."

"Thank you, sir."

"Shame you had to leave the teams, but I understand why."

"Thank you, sir," he repeated, the knot tugging at his gut. "Initially, I took leave, hoping to rejoin my team after my dad got better. But it appears that's going to take a while, so I had to retire." His whole body tensed. Damn, he hadn't realized how much it hurt to say out loud. He drew in a breath and let it out slowly.

"What if I told you there was still a way to help out this country?"

Matteo stiffened. "How, sir?"

He sure as hell wasn't going to sling pizza the rest of his life.

"I'd like to add you to the sleeper cells I'm creating from retired SEALs."

A sliver of adrenaline materialized and kicked up his pulse. "Sleeper SEALs?"

"Exactly. Are you interested?"

Hell, yeah. The lightness in his chest, and his suddenly dry mouth were signs of affirmation, but the timing sucked. "I am, sir, but I need to sort out what happened to my dad."

"You're concerned about the sequence of the head trauma," Lambert said, with agreement underlying his tone.

Matteo didn't bother to ask how much detail the commander knew about his father's stroke, or how. The answer was probably above his pay grade.

When he'd had one.

"Yes," he replied, and went on to quickly explain his concern. "Could be nothing. But I need to know."

"Understandable," Lambert said. "And this happened when? Three weeks ago?"

Something in the man's tone set the hair on Matteo's neck on end. "Yes. Why? Could this be related to the reason you called?"

"I don't know. Like you said, could be nothing."

"Or it could be something," he countered, everything inside him screaming that it was. All the more reason for him to take the mission.

Even if it wasn't related, the job would keep him from going stark-raving mad from slinging pizza all day. Or dealing with the holiday hype already sweeping through the boardwalk shops, commandeering the local radio stations, and abuzz in customers' conversations. He hated this time of the year. Between the commercialism, and growing up with Santa in his last name…yeah, Matteo definitely fell into the Grinch category.

"Tell me about the mission." He already knew he'd say yes.

"I know I don't have to ask if you've heard of Rasheed Al-Zahawi."

"Fuck, no." Matteo's heart slammed into the floor at the same time his gaze sought Bella on the security monitor. She stood by the counter, pizza in her hand and smile on her face, captivating a grinning Joe with something she was saying. Her life had changed irreparably because of Rasheed. She'd suffered because of him, and Matteo had vowed to someday find the man and make him pay. "You should've started your pitch with that."

"Guess I should've." Lambert's tone was as grim as the thoughts rushing through Matteo's head. "I know your godfather was killed trying to stop Rasheed from carrying out another attack on New York City."

"He did stop him," Matteo pointed out, damn proud of Bella's father for saving thousands of lives that fateful New Year's Eve, thirteen years ago.

"Yes, he did, at the sacrifice of his own life," the commander said. "Damn shame no one knew he'd saved Times Square, and countless lives."

Over a million people had been in attendance that night. Matteo remembered his father telling him that in order to keep the city from panicking, the authorities kept the thwarted plot, and all mention of terrorists—captured, killed, or escaped—out of the media.

His gaze returned to Bella again. "Those who mattered to him, knew."

"Well, there's chatter Rasheed's back in the states, headed for your city, if he isn't there already."

Shit. Matteo straightened up. "He's coming to Atlantic City?"

"Yes. Word is, he has sympathizers there, already in place, prepping for his arrival. Which is any day."

"How reliable is your intel?"

"Very. We got it from Samir Al-Jamil."

Damn. Matteo's chest tightened. Those two assholes were involved in several attacks together.

"Samir said he was planning to, and I quote, 'Make sure America has a reason not to forget your holidays.' He said Rasheed was involved and someone else Rasheed kept a secret. Chatter is, it could be one of the FBI's top three most wanted."

Heavy hitters. He ran a hand through his hair. "Why isn't Homeland handling this?"

"Since we don't know the exact target, other than the city, and we don't know all the players, we need to be careful. Can't have a ton of agents crawling around, spooking the cell before we know the venue and everyone involved. The bastards will scatter only to come back in the distant future to finish the attack. No. We need you to locate those sympathizers, and Rasheed, find out the venue and who else is involved."

"So, this isn't a capture and kill."

"No. Not yet. We need Rasheed alive," Lambert stated. "Sorry. I get that you'd want blood."

Damn straight. For what that bastard had put Bella and her mother through? Before the woman had died in a car accident a few years later. His father had suffered, too. Losing a buddy in combat was bad enough, but to survive the Gulf War, only to be taken out while protecting the innocent in the states had hit his father hard. So, yeah, damn right Matteo wanted blood.

He'd killed for his country before. It didn't mean he liked it, but he carried out his orders and moved on, otherwise, it could cripple his psyche and render him useless. But some missions, like this one, he welcomed a CAK order.

Too bad this wasn't one of them.

"Unfortunately, Rasheed is too valuable to kill right now." The commander's voice held an undercurrent of disgust. "Doesn't mean someone won't try. You're going to have to make sure that doesn't happen."

Great. "The government hasn't put the word out to all the agencies that he has information on an impending attack?"

"Sure they have, but that doesn't guarantee they'll all listen. That's why it's imperative that you get your hands on him first. Lives are at stake, Santarelli. You must locate these men and find out what they're planning."

"And then what, sir? Do I contact you? Do I have backup?" Seemed like too high-profile a target to let it all fall on one retired SEAL. Not that he couldn't handle it.

"Officially, no," Lambert said. "This is an unsanctioned op, so if you're caught, you're on your own. The U.S. Government won't bail your ass out, or take any responsibility."

Nothing new.

"Once you locate Rasheed and extract the information, then call me. I'll pass the information on to the pertinent agencies, as well as let you know if your orders change."

Matteo stood a little taller at the unspoken confidence in the commander's tone and words. "Roger that."

"If you find you do require backup then consider calling Knight. His agency doesn't answer to subcommittees, so he can offer immediate assistance."

He nodded as if Lambert had a visual on him. "Will do," he said. "Circling back to my dad, sir. Earlier, you alluded that perhaps this mission had something to do with my father. How?"

"I don't believe in coincidences," the commander answered. "The fact your father suffered a blow to the head — whether naturally or unnaturally — around the same time chatter started about sympathizers preparing for

Rasheed, seems a bit too convenient. It makes my damn nose hair twitch. Plus, if you factor in your father's overall good health, and lack of medication, it all points to foul play. Hell, I'm on cholesterol medication and high blood pressure pills, and according to your dad's medical records, he doesn't take a Goddamn one."

A smile tugged Matteo's lips. Leave it to his father to frustrate the commander without a face-to-face. And the fact Lambert got his hands on his dad's medical records proved the commander had high-level clearance.

"Never doubt your gut, Santarelli. It got you through many missions," Lambert pointed out. "You felt something was off, and I agree with you."

Roger that. "So it's possible he may have heard something, or seen something."

"Or someone," Lambert added. "Your father's lucky to be alive. You know how these bastards work. They don't leave witnesses."

Invisible, cold fingers squeezed Matteo's heart, sending chills down his spine. "They were probably interrupted."

Even though it was a slower time of year, the boardwalk still drew a crowd in spurts.

"Most likely."

Fuck. Those cold fingers squeezed harder. His dad was a sitting duck. Thank God he'd at least had the foresight to restrict visitors to family. But if these people wanted his father dead, they'd find a way to get in.

"Now that I think about it," Lambert said. "I'm going to call Jameson and ask him to provide protection for your dad. His agents are former SEALs and military, so don't worry, your father will be safe at the center, and can continue his rehab. This way you can work this mission without worrying about him. Plus, they could provide backup, should you need it."

"I appreciate that, sir," he said, already feeling the tightness ease in his chest.

He'd be able to work cleaner, smarter, quicker if he wasn't worried about his father.

"A few more things before I go. Make sure you check in with me. You can use this number you called. And as for your compensation," the commander said, mentioning an amount which equaled a fuck-ton of money.

But he didn't give a rat's ass if he got paid. Matteo wasn't doing it for money. He took the mission for his dad. For Bella. For his godfather, and to bring justice to his killer…after he extracted the information he needed to shut down the cell and ensure no one died on his watch.

Something about the commander's silence unsettled his gut. "Why do I get the impression there's something else, sir?"

Lambert's chuckle filled his ear. "Because you're a damn good SEAL."

Was...

His unsettled gut tightened, and he considered correcting the man, but changed his mind. Lambert was right. Matteo would never stop being a SEAL. He'd earned his trident, fought for his country. Took bullets for his brothers. No one could take any of that away from him.

"You also need a heads-up," Lambert stated. "There's chatter that a few agencies have sanctioned a hit on Rasheed."

"Foreign?"

"And domestic," Lambert replied. "So locate those sympathizers, find Rasheed, and get that bastard to talk before he can't."

Matteo nodded. "Yes, sir."

"I'm going to call Jameson now. Expect to hear from him soon," Lambert told him, before hanging up.

After clicking off the phone, Matteo sank into the chair behind the desk and blew out a breath. Fucking terrorist sympathizers might've attacked his dad.

The same questions from before ran through his mind. Why didn't they kill him? Were they interrupted? Did his father know his attacker? Did the attacker know his dad survived?

He was hoping against hope that none of that mattered because his father's stroke was brought on by natural causes.

Not that he wished bad health on his father, but the alternative was harder to swallow. He would have enough on his plate trying to find Rasheed and keep the prick alive.

Damn. He couldn't believe he had to protect the bastard. And from American, and probably foreign agents, no doubt. His gaze wandered to Bella's sweet image on the monitor again.

How the hell would she feel knowing the man who killed her father was coming to Atlantic City, or possibly already here, and he had to keep the guy safe?

His stomach lurched as he imagined her smile fading, and brows crashing together from the disappointment rippling through her body.

Good thing she wasn't going to know.

Chapter Three

Instinctively, Bella knew Matteo's phone call was about Rasheed Al-Zahawi. So why the hell was she out here in the restaurant?

What she should've done was sat her ass in a chair and stayed until he asked her to leave, or planted one of the several listening devices stored in her backpack. But instead, she left him alone to talk to someone Jameson knew, about the man who killed her dad.

She was a fool, and too damn soft where Matteo was concerned. He muddled her mind. Kept her from doing her job. Dammit.

Rasheed was *her* mark. *Her* sanctioned hit. She couldn't allow feelings for her childhood crush to screw up her mission. Her *life-long* mission to remove Rasheed's evil from the world.

Of course, she hadn't stood idly by, eating pizza and gabbing to Joe, either. A quick text to her friend Brooke, who worked for Jameson Knight at the Knight Agency, netted her the identity of Matteo's caller.

Commander Greg Lambert.

Admiration warmed her blood. Admiration for the commander and his achievements known throughout her circle of peers, and for Matteo and the fact a great leader like Lambert sought him out.

No surprise. The guy always gave a hundred and ten percent. He didn't know how to fail.

She bit into her pizza, enjoying the combination of fresh mozzarella and marinara on a thin crust, with just the right thickness and hint of garlic that made her mouth water. Dammit. Even his pies were exceptional.

Taking another bite, she thought about her conversation with Joe, about things that happened while she was away. A rash of recent break-ins among a few shops on the boardwalk, and in town, a missing boat and a fire in an abandoned building. Were they relevant? Maybe not, but she was going to check them out...after she saw her godfather.

But she'd have to wait for Matteo to take her, since Joe also told her only family was allowed to visit.

Smart move.

A prickling at the base of her neck spread out to bite across her shoulders. If someone cold-cocked him, they were going to beg to be arrested.

"Bella, you ready?" Matteo's deep, delicious tone turned the prickling to tingling across her shoulders.

She turned, and noted he'd donned a black leather jacket over his red *Santarelli Pizza* T-shirt, and damn, she enjoyed the view of all six foot one of incredible, lethal, confident, muscle striding her way. The tingle grew to a shiver as his dark gaze remained on her, warming parts that normally stayed frozen.

Good or bad? Jury was still out.

"Always," she replied, receiving a sexy grin that shifted her heart.

Okay. Bad. Definitely bad.

She didn't need the man messing with that organ. Again. Last time, she willingly offered it to him, only to receive a refusal.

No thank you.

No matter how damn hot he was, or how much her body longed to feel that sexy stubble graze her skin. Dammit.

She tossed her plate in the trash, swiped her drink off the counter, and proceeded to suck down the last of her lemonade. All was going well, until he made a strangled noise, and she glanced to find his gaze on her mouth.

A flood of awareness hit her body, jolting it awake, concentrating on her neglected areas, until she was ready to either smack him, or ride him. Deciding to do neither, she listened to the devil on her shoulder and sucked harder, louder, then slowly removed the straw from her mouth, before throwing the cup away.

Yeah, she was bad. Downright wicked, even, because she walked straight for him, smiled up into his dazed face, and reached out to grab her satellite phone he gripped near his hip. "Ready."

Without waiting for a reply, she turned around and nodded to Joe as she stuffed the phone into her backpack on her way to the door.

"We're going to see my dad," Matteo told Joe, right on her six. "Russell should be in soon." Reaching around her to open the door, he leaned close and whispered in her ear, "Be careful, Bella. You shouldn't play with fire."

Ignoring him would've been the smart thing. Yep. Ignore him and keep walking through the door, but did she listen? No. Instead, she listened to the damn devil on her shoulder again, who continued to give bad advice, because she stopped dead, causing Matteo to crash the front of his hard, rigid body into her back.

Operating on awareness overload, she trembled as she turned her head to glance over her shoulder at him, telling herself she didn't love the feel of that delicious stubble brushing her face. "Marines don't play...*Frogman*."

With that, Bella pushed the door open the rest of the way and stepped out onto the boardwalk, welcoming the sharp wind blowing off the Atlantic. The cold air slapped the stupid from her brain, cooled her neglected libido, and restored her focus.

Was her stupid, idiotic teenage persona going to rear its hopeless head around Matteo the whole damn time he was near? God, she hoped not. It was damned embarrassing, and dangerous to the success of her assignment.

Killing Rasheed was her mission. Not flirting with Matteo.

Drawing in a good, deep lungful of the magic air, she slung her backpack over her shoulder and walked next to an equally composed former SEAL. Together, they nodded to Omar and two of his sons, Paresh and Jalil, as they passed his sundry shop. The Guptas had been around for as long as Bella could remember. Her dad and Matteo's, used to go deep-sea fishing every spring. Back when the world was a fairy tale and nightmares didn't exist.

Now, they were a way of life and fairy tales were fiction.

"Thanks again, for the use of your phone," Matteo said, snapping her out of her melancholy, as they turned the corner to head down the ramp toward the parking lot.

She shrugged, and decided to do a little fishing herself. "No problem. I take it you had a good conversation?"

Now he shrugged. "Yeah." He cupped her elbow and nodded toward the lot behind the buildings. "I'm parked here."

"So, is there a reason we went around the buildings instead of using the back door in Santarelli's?" she asked, trying to dissuade her heart from fluttering as he led her to a sexy black Charger, but failed when he unlocked and opened the passenger door for her.

Sweet man.

Stupid organ.

"Yes," he replied, after getting in and starting the car. "I wanted a quick peek inside Omar's shop."

Omar's?

A heavy feeling settled in her stomach. "Why? Because of the phone call? Or your dad?" Either way, she decided it wasn't good.

Turning to face him, she studied his profile while he drove through town, noting his hunched shoulders and dark circles beneath his eyes from his obvious lack of sleep. And worry.

He lifted a shoulder. "It sucks. I know," he said, steering wheel creaking in his tight grasp. "But, until I find out what really happened, I'm conditioned to think the worst. So…everybody's suspect."

She sighed. "I agree. We aren't taking any chances with your dad."

His gaze snapped to hers, and a slight twinkle lightened the dark depths. "We?"

"Damn straight." She smiled. "If anyone hurt him, they're going to have to answer to me, too."

"After I spend some quality time with them."

"Of course," she said. "Mr. Frogman. Sir."

He chuckled, and the sound sent a damn zing spiraling through her chest, cracking the shell surrounding her heart. His eyes continued to sparkle. "You can call me Master Chief. Or just…Master."

Laughter burst from her chest, echoing through the car as she worked to catch her breath. "That's a good one. I'd tell you to kiss my ass, but I have a feeling you'd enjoy that too much."

"So would you," he murmured in a low, sexy tone. "Believe me, baby. So would you."

And just like that, all the amusement warming her veins switched to arousal, turning her blood into liquid heat. She shifted in her seat and told her good parts to forget it. They'd never get a shot at him. The man was just playing. He'd never go against his father's wishes.

Although, she doubted his dad would have a problem with them getting together now that she was well out of her teens. Still, things were different now. *She* was different now. Matteo deserved better. It wasn't worth the pursuit.

Deciding not to fight a losing battle, Bella didn't bother to reply, and changed the subject instead. "Did you notice anything amiss at Omar's shop?"

"No," he replied, turning into the parking lot of the Atlantic Rehabilitation Medical Center. "Half of me is relieved, but the other half is frustrated as hell." Muttering under his breath, he pulled into a spot and jammed the car in park, "If only the stubborn fool had put an actual security system in place."

Without thinking, Bella reached out to set her hand on his shoulder and squeeze. "We'll figure it out."

He nodded, and released the steering wheel to set his hand on her knee, as if the reaction was as natural as breathing. Exactly how it felt. Natural. A comfort, not a sexual advance. She wasn't even tempted to break his hand, like she would've with anyone else who touched her there without an invitation.

"Bella." He sat there, staring at her with his mouth open as if he wanted to tell her something, a flicker of guilt clouding his gaze. But then he blinked, and it was gone. "We should go in," he said, releasing her to grab his keys.

What the hell was that all about?

Unsure she even wanted to know, she nodded. "Can you pop the trunk? I'd like to leave my backpack."

Weapons weren't usually required inside a hospital, and if they happened to have security set up to search bags, she wasn't in the mood to explain her stash.

"Sure." He hit a button on the lower left side of his dash, and a soft thud sounded a second before the trunk opened.

"Thanks." She got out, tossed her pack inside, and slammed the trunk shut, before joining him on the sidewalk in front of his car. "Maybe you should tell me what to expect." There were different types of strokes, and different levels of damage.

His sigh fogged the cold air as they walked toward the entrance. "Just imagine the worst. His speech is slurred and he can't walk."

The worst was losing your father. His was alive, which was a gift. Anything else her godfather could overcome. "Yet," she said, meeting his gaze as he held the door open for her. "He's too stubborn to stay that way."

A smile tugged his lips. "True." After he signed them in at the front desk, he cupped her elbow and led her down a corridor where he took a left, and then a right, before stopping at a private room. "Just remember, it's like you said. He won't always be like this."

Before anxiety had a chance to settle in her belly, he tugged her into the room.

Chapter Four

Bella thought she'd prepared herself. After all, it wasn't like she hadn't seen plenty of men paralyzed before. Hell, half of them were at her hands. But they were terrorists, and murderers who raped and massacred, with no regard for human life.

Not an honorable man who stepped into the role of father when she lost hers. A strong, funny man, who volunteered as a firefighter, coached a little league team, taught English to immigrants at night at the community center.

A heaviness settled over her shoulders, weighing down into her chest as she approached the big man lying in the bed.

"Look who I ran into today, Dad," Matteo said, standing next to her.

Bella wasn't sure what she'd expected, but it wasn't to see Angelo Santarelli looking...normal? The fifty-five-year-old appeared just as fit and imposing as ever. His face wasn't twisted, nor was any part of his body. The only evidence of something off was the scar in the salt-n-pepper hairline near his right temple.

But then he tried to talk. "B-ba...B-ba..." He threw his body back and forth, as if trying to sit up. His frustrated growl echoed through the room.

"It's all right, Dad. Calm down. I'll help you sit up," Matteo stated, doing just that, with her help.

Once they raised the bed, and her godfather was settled into a sitting position, she studied him carefully, watching the muscles in his face as he tried to speak again.

"N-n-na...n-n-na..." Color flooded his cheeks, and his dark eyes flashed his impatience. "N-n-ne..."

An inkling of an idea manifested in her head, too crazy to be real. And yet... "Matteo, tell me exactly what the doctor said. Is there evidence of a stroke? A bleed on the brain? Both?"

"Subdural hematoma from the head injury, and ischemic stroke caused by a blood clot," he replied. "But he got to the hospital within the first three hours, so they were able to treat him quickly and prevent it from getting worse."

"Was the clot caused by the injury?"

"No one knows."

She studied her godfather, noting his flared nostrils and several grunts.

"N-n-na...n-n-ne," he muttered again, rocking sideways slightly.

That inkling turned into a gnawing. He should've made better progress by now. She turned and headed for the door. "Close the blinds," she told Matteo, and shut the door before flicking off the lights.

"What the hell?" he grumbled in the darkened room.

Her lips twitched. He never was crazy about the dark.

"Bear with me." She pulled the phone from her pocket and tapped the flashlight app on her way back to the bed, and a soft glow filled the room. Sitting on the edge of the bed, she aimed the light at her godfather's face, then moved it off to the side to observe his pupils.

Shit. Her heart dropped to her stomach. They dilated. Both times. She knew why he wasn't improving. Hell, she should...she worked with toxins enough to recognize the symptoms.

Angelo Santarelli was poisoned.

***

Matteo scratched his temple as he leaned against the wall and watched Bella flick light into his father's eyes. Why was she checking his dilation? What was she looking for? She wasn't a doctor. How did she even know to check…whatever the hell she was checking?

Her back stiffened.

"What is it?" he asked, straightening from the wall.

She jumped to her feet. "You can open the blinds," she said, heading for the door, flicking the lights on as she passed. "I'll be right back."

Before he could question her further she was gone. He glanced at his dad, and could swear he saw a ghost of a smile tugging his lips. "Never could get a straight answer from her," he muttered. "Why should today be any different?"

"Any different for what?" she asked, breezing back in, clutching something in her hand as she re-approached the bed.

Stepping close, he frowned. "Mind telling me what's going on?"

"Don't need to. Your dad will. Sort of."

She was way too cryptic and mysterious for his liking. "Bella, what the hell's going on?"

Ignoring him, she stared at his dad and sat on the edge of the bed again. "I noticed you can blink your eyes. So, I need you to blink once for yes, and twice for no. Okay?"

His dad blinked once.

A rock, the size of his fist, felt like it settled in the pit of his stomach. Fuck. He'd never thought to try that to communicate with his dad. All this time…

"Good. Now, is this what you're trying to say?" She uncurled her fist to reveal a syringe in the palm of her hand.

"N-n-na...n-n-ne," his dad uttered as he blinked. Once.

What the hell?

That rock in Matteo's gut grew three sizes. He stepped right to the bed. "Someone stuck you with a needle?"

Again, his father blinked once.

"Did you see who it was?" Bella asked, because she at least had some brain function.

Blame it on the shock muddling his brain, or the anger heating his blood—which sucked all the oxygen from said muddled brain—either way, he wasn't thinking clearly.

Two blinks.

Damn. His dad hadn't seen the culprit. "What the hell could they have stuck in him? And why didn't the doctors catch it?"

"Some kind of neurotoxin," she replied. "And no one would catch it unless they were looking for it. I doubt poison is part of a stroke screening."

True. But...damn. This was just nuts.

More questions filled his mind. Like, what kind of poison was it? How was the toxin still in his father's system? Who administered it? And just how the hell did Bella know so much about neurotoxins?

But before he could ask, a knock sounded as the door opened and Jameson Knight entered, with a woman similar in height, coloring, and attitude as Bella.

"Commander Knight." Matteo walked forward to shake his former commander's hand. "It's been a long time, sir. Glad you could make it on such short notice."

Now, more than ever, he was relieved to have protection for his father, especially someone as capable and trustworthy as Knight. After earning his Budweiser, by completing BUDs, Army Airborne School, SEAL AOT, and a probationary period, Matteo was assigned to Knight's team—per Knight's request.

For two years, he served under the commander, until the CIA lured Knight into their elite Special Operations Group. He'd heard the guy did several years there, before leaving to start his own agency. The one Lambert had mentioned on the phone earlier.

"Good to see you, too, Reaper," Knight replied, cupping his shoulder as he shook his hand. "Sorry it's for these reasons."

"And what reasons would that be?" Bella asked, stepping close enough that he was forced to release Knight's hand and move out of the way, so she could...hug the commander?

What the fuck?

"Ah, Bella. Always a pleasure." Knight grinned, as she kissed his cheek. "You ready to come work for me yet?"

"Photojournalist my ass," he muttered, and received three snickers.

It all made sense. The backpack. Satellite phone. Her trips out of the country. The way she carried herself with a capable, lethal grace.

Holy shit. Bella worked for Knight.

She drew back and smiled at the commander. "Not sure your agency could handle both me and Brooke."

Or…maybe not.

Knight introduced him to Brooke, the woman Bella was releasing from a hug, then nodded to his dad. "Gunny, I promise you we'll get things cleared up."

It didn't surprise Matteo that Knight knew his father was a Marine Gunnery Sergeant in the Gulf War. But it did surprise him that he'd arrived so fast. "Did you fly up, sir?"

Knight nodded. "Yes. Brooke is always eager to fly instead of drive."

Bella muttered something and shared a grin with the woman. He didn't even bother to try to dissect the meaning.

"So, how about you fill us in?" Knight leaned against the wall and folding his arms across his chest. "You looked alarmed and Bella looked disturbed when we walked in. Did you find evidence that your dad was attacked?"

"Yes," he replied, anger washing through him in another wave of heat. He swiped the needle from the table and waved it at them. "From this, not a blow to the head, as I originally suspected. Dad just confirmed someone used a needle on him."

Brooke frowned, stepping closer. "That one?"

"No." He shook his head. "Bella brought it in to question my dad."

Who the hell knew where she got it.

Bella's shoulders dropped with her sigh. "Nothing goes that easy." She went on to explain what she did with the lights, and her findings. "I don't have a reverse agent. The toxins I've worked with don't impair speech."

Knight pushed from the wall and moved close. "I'll have our guy test Gunny's blood to detect exactly what was used, and determine the correct reverse agent."

Matteo hoped to God it wasn't too late.

"Any chance your guy can trace it back the manufacturer so I can pay him, or her, a visit?" He was already visualizing his hands around the bastard's neck...after he got the name and location of the person who ordered the toxin.

"A damn good chance." Knight grinned. "Our guy's good. I'll let you know what we find out. In the meantime, Brooke and I will move your dad somewhere safe, so you can concentrate on other things." The commander gave him a pointed look.

Yeah. Like Rasheed.

Although he tried not to, Matteo couldn't stop his damn gaze from shifting to Bella. She quirked a brow, but said nothing.

For once.

Her odd behavior niggled at him, but he didn't have time to ponder it. "Thank you, sir," he said instead. "Before you move my dad, there are a few things I need to ask him. He's been communicating with blinks. One for yes, two for no." Matteo moved to stand by his father's shoulder and held his gaze. "Were there people in the shop when it happened?"

One blink.

Now the hard question. "Omar?"

Two blinks.

Relief disintegrated the tightness gripping his chest, but after naming several more names of workers and regulars, and continuing to get two blinks, the tightness returned. Dammit. Who the hell had been in there?

Bella walked close. "Were there three people?"

Two blinks.

"Two people?" he asked.

One blink.

Finally. Now they were getting somewhere.

Bella shifted her feet. "Do you know them?"

One…no, two…wait, three blinks?

"So, you know one but not the other?" he asked, and received an affirmative, with one blink. He glanced at Bella. "Who haven't we asked about?"

She lifted a shoulder. "I'm not sure. Maybe someone new showed up while I was gone."

One blink.

"How about family?" Brooke asked from behind, and his dad blinked once.

Matteo reeled back, his heart diving into his gut. "Our family?"

No way. His sister and Joe would never do anything like this.

His dad grunted. "N-n-n…" And blinked twice.

"Someone else's family member." Knight's suggestion garnered a solo blink.

He stiffened as a sudden certainty washed over him. "Paresh?"

One blink.

"Damn." Omar's oldest son. He ran a hand through his hair and blew out a breath, already dreading what he knew it meant he had to do.

"Did he hit you? Did anyone hit you?" Bella fired off two questions, and received two single blinks. "So the person with Paresh gave you the injection?"

Another affirmative blink.

"His brother, Jalil?" Matteo closed his eyes and sighed after he received two blinks for a no.

Thank God, because he was still having a hard time accepting the fact either of Omar's sons could be involved.

Hell, his dad coached both of them for years. Held birthday parties in the shop for them. Invited them over for barbeques. It was insane.

What the hell could cause someone you knew his whole life to turn on you?

"Was it a young male around Paresh's age?" Bella asked.

He opened his eyes in time to see his dad blink once. No doubt, the kid was one of the sympathizers Commander Lambert mentioned. Exactly the person he needed to talk to.

Time for a body snatch.

But first, he needed to make sure his dad was safe. As Bella and Brooke continued to question his father, Matteo walked over to Knight, who was just shoving his phone back in his pocket. "You said you had someone who could help figure out what they injected into my dad?"

"Yes," Knight replied. "But we're going to need to fly him down to D.C."

"When?"

"Today. I've already got my people on it." Knight patted his pocket. "They started the transfer paperwork. Should have it within the hour. It'll require your signature."

"Then what?"

"Brooke and I will fly your dad down to a secure complex where a team of specialists are standing by to get this sorted out," Knight said. "Once he's settled in, Brooke and I will fly back to assist with…your other problem."

Even though he and the commander were speaking in hushed tones, Matteo glanced over at the bed to see if the others caught that last part—mainly Bella—but he needn't worry, because she was gone.

"Where's Bella?" He frowned at Brooke.

The woman shrugged. "She left a minute ago. Said something about putting money in a meter so her car wasn't towed."

Shit. Alarm ricocheted through his chest. "She came here with me. In my car."

Knight's lips twitched. "You're not parked by a meter, are you?"

"No."

"Does she know this Paresh kid?" Brooke asked.

Fuck. He headed for the door. "I'll be back to sign those papers."

Matteo rushed through the building, with Brooke hot on his six, and together they burst out into the parking lot. He surveyed the area for signs of the impulsive woman, but saw none.

Until he approached his car. "Son-of-a-bitch."

The window of the driver side door was smashed in. Shards of glass littered the front seat, along with a hastily scribbled note.

Needed to pop the trunk to get my bag. Sorry for the mess. I'll pay for it. P.S. Careful you don't cut yourself on the glass.

"Dammit." He was too late.

A soft chuckle sounded behind him. He turned to find Brooke standing with a smile on her lips.

"She likes you."

His brows crashed together. What the hell did that have to do with anything? Even though it was irrelevant to the mission, he couldn't stop his mouth from voicing a non-mission related question. "How can you tell?"

"By the very fact she left you a note." Brooke's grin grew lopsided. "Trust me. That's not her style."

Matteo didn't even want to know how this woman knew what Bella's style was. "A note?" He wrenched open the door and pointed to the mess inside. "Did you see what she did to my car?"

"Yeah. You're lucky," she said.

This woman was as crazy as Bella. "Why am I lucky?"

"Because she left you the car."

True.

Hope flickered through his chest and turned into a rush of adrenaline. She couldn't have gotten far. He popped the trunk to grab a mini dustpan and brush, and quickly cleared the glass from his seat. Why the hell didn't she wait for him? Christ, he hoped the impetuous woman didn't screw things up.

Some things never changed. Grunting, he tossed the glass-filled pan and brush on the passenger floor, before getting in. Apparently, the Marine Corps didn't squash her impulsiveness.

He glanced at Brooke as he started the engine. "Tell Knight I'll be back to sign those papers."

She stepped back and nodded. "Good luck."

What he needed was restraint, because Bella deserved a good spanking and he was just the person to give her one.

Chapter Five

She should've taken the damn car.

It was official. She was going soft.

Bella opened the throttle on the Vespa, she commandeered down the street from the rehab center, and barely hit 40 mph. Call it wishful thinking, she remained in the fast lane anyway. Christ, she could run faster.

Dammit. Matteo always was her Achilles heel.

Not only did she *not* take his car, she left a damn note — and said she was sorry.

What the freakin' hell?

Cruising down Atlantic Avenue, she inhaled the cold air, then exhaled slowly, working to regain her calm when a car pulled up on her right and slowed down to keep pace with her piece of crap ride. She knew who it was before glancing over.

Sexy, smartass Santarelli.

Sure enough, he waved at her through his broken window. A sliver of guilt flickered in her belly, until his lips tugged into a lop-sided grin.

"Careful," he said. "You might blow a gasket."

She flipped him off, and could hear his chuckle echo in the wind as he left her in his wake—by doing the damn speed limit.

But she refused to let it get to her. She had more important things to worry about. Like finding Paresh.

Although she wanted to wring the fool's neck, Bella planned to let the kid lead her to his friend, then let that bastard lead her to Rasheed. She knew in her gut that was where all this was leading.

By the time she parked up the street from the community basketball courts, and gladly jumped off the Vespa, Bella found her calm again. Paresh and his brother always shot hoops after Jalil got out of school. With luck, they were still there.

She approached the teenager and his two buddies, noting a black Charger up the street with a busted driver's side window and a frogman behind the wheel. Grasping the chain-link fence, she leaned into the cold metal and smiled at the boys through the slats. "Hey, Jalil. Is your brother here?"

Waving, the kid moved closer. "Nah. Paresh stopped coming here." His gaze dropped to the court, before lifting to meet hers, sadness and anger mixing to cloud the dark depths. "He's too busy with his new friends to hang out with us anymore."

"I'm sorry to hear that." More than Jalil knew.

"Jalil? Toss the ball, man," one of his friends called, while the other clapped and held out his hands.

He turned and tossed the ball to his friends, before twisting back to face her. "I'm sorry, too."

"Do you happen to know where he hangs out now? They're supposed to start hiring at the Capris again, and he asked me to let him know," she added to lessen suspicion. It was semi-true. Paresh had asked her...last year.

"No. We don't talk like we used to," the teenager stated. "He's kind of a dick. Like his friends Tariq and Kamal."

Bingo. The names she wanted.

A smile tugged her lips. "You don't like them much, huh?"

"No. And I don't like Paresh much lately, either. Not since he started hanging out with them. Those guys are as fake as their names. They aren't even Middle Eastern. They're as white as..." His voice trailed off as color rose into his cheeks.

"As me?" She smiled. "It's okay. I get it. And I'm sorry. Maybe I can talk to him. You sure you don't have any idea where he may be?"

Shifting his feet, he pursed his lips and squinched his eyes as if deep in thought. "I did see him go into that abandoned building on 5th Street once." He shrugged. "Maybe they hang out there."

"Maybe." She kept her features neutral despite the adrenaline rushing through her body. An abandoned building. Joe had mentioned one in conjunction with a fire. Not the same one, but it could still be connected. Perhaps the sympathizers sought a new one after the fire. One way to find out. It was now her destination. "Thanks, Jalil. I won't keep you any longer. Go sink some threes."

"You know it." Smiling, he turned and rushed across the court toward his buddies.

He was a good kid. So was Paresh—at that age.

What could've happened to make him fall in with terrorist sympathizers?

Bella contemplated that as she walked down the street, past the piece-of-crap Vespa and turned at the corner. Most converts had low self-esteem, wanted to belong, to matter. Paresh came from loving parents who always put their kids first. It made no sense.

Although, neither did terrorism. Not to her.

Pulling the collar up on her jacket, she ducked her head against the wind on her way down the block. If Paresh was indeed mixed up with the cell, and unreachable, she wouldn't hesitate to turn him in.

"Bella, get in," Matteo said through the rolled down window on the passenger side of his car, as he coasted along with her. "Come on. It's cold out."

"You don't want to warm me up, Matteo. You just want to know where I'm headed," she said, before stopping.

So did he.

Unable to stop the smile from spreading across her face, she stepped close to lean in the window. "How about I tell you where I'm going?"

She loved a good challenge. It might be fun to race him.

His brows slammed together. "How about you get in the damn car?"

Unwanted arousal shot to her core. "So forceful." Extremely aware of her increased heartbeats and the warmth flooding her body, she lifted a hand to stroke her neck, and grinned. "Are you going to make me?"

Bella knew she shouldn't mess with him. Finding Paresh and his new friends was more important, but damn, she couldn't help herself. Never could. Not where Matteo was concerned.

"Damn straight." His nostrils flared and gaze flashed with a heat she felt down to her toes.

"It's rather cute how you think you'd succeed."

"Bella," he growled, in a low, gravelly voice that made her insides quiver. "Get. In. This. Car. Now." The vein in his neck bulged and throbbed in unison with his flexing, white-knuckled grip on the steering wheel.

Taking pity on him, she got in, mindful of the pile of glass on the floor. "Fine. Since you asked nicely."

And also because her damn knees had actually weakened under the force of the arousal he awoke inside her.

Not good.

"Care to tell me where we're going?" He lifted a brow, which only added to his overwhelming sex appeal.

As if he needed more.

Bastard.

She snorted. "A one-way trip on the crazy train."

He turned to face her but instead of a grumpy retort, he snickered. "We always did have season passes."

"True."

They smiled at each other, until the seconds turned into a minute and their amusement switched to something fierce, rampant, and hot. So hot, the windshield started to fog—even with both windows open.

The urge to climb over the console, straddle the noticeable bulge protruding behind his zipper and take the kiss she'd dreamt about her whole life was so strong, Bella almost shifted toward him. But at the last second, common sense kicked in, and she ripped her gaze from him instead.

"Head to the abandoned building on 5th Street," she said, flicking the button to close her window. "That's where Jalil said his brother might be, with his two new friends."

Matteo muttered a curse and clicked on the defroster before shifting into drive. "Two?"

She nodded. "Yeah, Tariq and Kamal, who—according to Jalil—aren't Middle Eastern. They're as white as me."

"Shit."

Her sigh echoed his. "Yeah." She knew it meant it was a good likelihood Paresh was mixed up with the sympathizers.

Crossing her feet, she hit the dustpan, knocking shards of glass from the pile. "Sorry about your window." The words were out before she could stop them.

Seriously? It was bad enough she wrote a note. Now she had to go and say it, too? The man was way too dangerous to her self-control. She needed to be hard. Needed to suppress human decency in order to do her job. At times, it meant foregoing pleasantries and politeness. She worked hard to basically be a bitch.

Then along came a sexy blast from her past, and all that control got smashed into pieces like a busted window, allowing her subdued emotions to escape through the cracks.

"Wouldn't it have been easier to just wait for me?" He stared at her through those mesmerizing dark eyes, full of righteous indignation and a sliver of smug tossed in to make them gleam.

She lifted a shoulder. "I'm used to working alone."

Mostly.

"Then you need a new job," he said as if it were that simple.

As if she had no choice.

"I love my job," she told him honestly. Ridding the earth of terrorists—whether through jail, gun, or blade—making the world a little safer, one monster at a time, helped her sleep better at night. Of course, he probably thought she worked with Knight in some capacity, and on occasion, she did. But her main job was through Homeland, and off the books. "I prefer to work alone. It's better. More efficient."

He pulled to the curb, a block back from the abandoned building, shoved the car in park, and leaned close. "Bet I could change your mind."

Oh, he could change her mind about a lot of things. But she didn't want him to. "And I can change the subject," she replied, removing her cell phone from her pocket.

He tipped his head and frowned. "To?"

"To the fact Paresh and his two buddies are leaving." She snapped several photos of the trio getting into a truck down the block and driving off before texting them to Brooke. If she sent the photos to her boss, then a phone call would soon follow, and out of respect for Omar, Bella was trying to delay it until she had a chance to talk to his son. "You follow them, and I'll go inside to look for the toxin, and to bug the place."

Grabbing them would alert Rasheed, and the bastard wouldn't show. But if they listened in, hopefully, in a day or so, Kamal and Tariq would give up details on Rasheed's arrival.

"Negatory," Matteo said. "We'll both go inside. The place is no doubt booby trapped. I'm not letting you go in alone."

"Okay. We'll cover more ground." Shifting forward, she shrugged out of her backpack and set it on her lap.

"Wait." He reeled back. "You agreed with me? Why aren't you arguing?"

A smile tugged her lips. "Would it help?"

"No."

"There's your answer." She removed a thermal imaging device to help her see inside the small office building. After a quick scan of all three floors revealed no heat signatures, she switched to scan for non-linear circuits. She found two.

"Good news is the building is empty. Bad news is there are two traps. One thru the front entrance at the top of the stairwell, and another in a room on the third floor." She pointed to the spots on the screen, and after he nodded, she powered it down before tucking it back in her bag. "We should power our cell phones down now, too."

After shutting her phone off, she shoved it back in her pocket while he did the same to his. They didn't need an ill-timed phone call to set off the bombs.

"So…what else do you have in your go bag?" He grinned when she snapped her gaze to his. "Yeah, I know a go bag when I see one. Mind telling me how you happen to have a thermal imager that also detects electronic circuits?"

Bella reached for the handle and got out of the car without responding.

A few seconds later he joined her, still wearing a slight grin as he leaned his back against her door. "Any chance you feel like telling me what your job is? You know, the one you love so much? And don't even think of trying to push that photojournalist bullshit on me."

Her laughter fogged the air in front of her as she slung her pack over her shoulder. "If I told you, I'd have to kill you. And I like you too much for that."

The latter was no secret. Unfortunately, she made that all too clear in her youth.

His chuckle increased the fog surrounding them. "Good to know."

"What? That I'd have to kill you?"

"No," he replied. "That you like me. Too much."

She snorted. "Don't let it go to your head. I have a soft spot for SEALs."

In a blink, he caged her between the hot muscles of his body and his car, slamming his hands on the roof on either side of her head. "What SEALs? How many? I want names."

His actions, his words, they caught Bella off-guard, suspending her breath as her heartbeat stuttered. What was he doing? Matteo never showed any emotion other than friendship, tolerance, or annoyance toward her. Until today. Damn man was messing with her mind. That's what he was doing. Messing big time, with his teasing, and flirting, and heated looks, and now this possessiveness?

Not a trait she'd tolerate with anyone, but damn, she'd be lying if she didn't admit it made her feel special, made her feel important to him.

Still. No one was ever going to own her.

Setting her palms on his chest, she brushed her thumbs over the cold leather of his jacket, feeling it heat between her hands and his hard body. "Be careful, frogman." She smiled into his serious face, more fascinated than she should be by the tight line of his lips and the way his nostrils flared again. "You're acting like you're jealous, and we both know that's silly, because you'd have to have feelings for me in order to be jealous."

He stiffened. "Are you serious? I've always had feelings for you, Bella. They didn't stop because I went to BUDs training."

Once again, her heartbeat stuttered. It was the first time he'd ever admitted having feelings for her — a decade too late.

"As always, your timing sucks, Matteo." Ignoring the urge to tug him close, she shoved him away instead, and stepped to the sidewalk. But she was under no illusion that it was all her doing. No. He'd let her go.

They were about to track down the bastard who'd poisoned his father, and could possibly lead them to the terrorist who killed her father. The last thing Bella wanted, or needed, was

Matteo distracting her with words and actions she'd longed for years ago.

If ever she needed to be on her A-game, it was now.

Slipping her backpack on her back, she approached the building, adrenaline rushing through her veins, warming her against the December cold. Of course, the arm Matteo slung around her shoulder might've had something to do with it, too.

"Put your arm around me, Bella. We don't want to draw attention to ourselves, if anyone happens to be watching," he said through a smile. "Better to appear to be lovers looking for some private time in the abandoned building than a pair about to bug the place."

She slid her hand around his back and gripped his hip. "True."

So was the tingling spreading down her right side as she brushed against his deliciously lean form. If anyone were to scan her with the thermal right now she'd light it up like the freaking Las Vegas strip.

"You good?" he asked, in a non-sexual tone and yet, her whole body screamed out a "hell, yeah" in response.

Stupid body. She cleared her throat. "I'd be better if we were inside." Where she could release him.

"Almost there." He chuckled, and dammit, she felt it vibrate right through her.

That was new.

And crazy—as if their attraction somehow magnified with age.

Not good. It'd been all-consuming in their youth. At least, on her end.

When they reached the door, he released her. "You're sure there aren't any proximity sensors or trip wires?"

She rolled her eyes, trying not to be insulted. "It's clear. I do know how to use a TI," she stated, holding up the imager.

Bastard grinned a sweet, sexy grin on those kissable lips of his. "Just playing it safe. Don't want to get us blown up before…" His voice trailed off and gaze dropped to her lips.

Maybe the cold wind was getting to her, or adrenaline, or the fact she was on the hunt for her father's killer. Whatever the reason, she was imagining things, because it felt like Matteo was flirting with her. Promising, alluding to them getting together.

Which was never on his agenda.

A second later, he turned back to the door. Yeah, her imagination was as rampant as the damn wind howling between the two buildings.

"Locked," he told her, digging in his coat pocket to produce a set of lock picks he used with a confidence and expertise that sent a thrill down her spine.

She kept that to herself as he opened the door and ushered her inside. The smell of stale air and dust made her nose itch.

"You sure there aren't any cameras?" he asked, glancing around the entrance full of graffiti tags and empty beer cans.

"Seriously?" Annoyance pricked her shoulders. She lifted the imager and scanned the area again. "Nope. Just the trip wire at the top of the stairs. See?" Holding the device out, she showed him on the monitor.

He gripped her shoulders and turned her to face him. "I'm sorry if you're insulted, but I'd rather you be pissed off than dead."

"Ah, you say the sweetest things." The tap she gave his cheek was meant to tease him—not her—but the feel of his soft beard made her want to rub more than her palm against his face.

And just like that, she wasn't cold anymore.

"I'm a sweet guy." He grinned.

Bella's snort echoed down the hall. "Humble, too."

"Of course. And I'm so humble and sweet, I'm going to let you help me check out this floor."

"Wow." She arched a brow as they headed down the hall. "Generous now, too. Consider my mind blown."

He grasped her arm and brought them to a stop. "You'll know when I blow your mind." Then he left her to search a room, while she stood with her heart thudding so loud it echoed down the hall.

Okay, so maybe her imagination wasn't playing tricks on her. She blinked, and took a few seconds to enjoy watching Matteo in SEAL mode. Stealthy, confident, thorough, he examined the room in under ten seconds.

Although watching him in his element made her hot, it also made Bella sad. Matteo was born to be a SEAL. She hated that he had to give it up because a Rasheed fan-boy attacked his dad.

If only she'd been in town and not off…doing the job she loved.

With a shake of her head and a sigh leading the way, she searched the three rooms on the other side of the hall. As expected, she found nothing but more empty beer cans and graffiti.

"Let's head upstairs," Matteo said, removing what looked like a pen from the inside of his coat, but when he pressed a button, it revealed the red beam of a laser pointer. "I'll take point."

She waved toward the stairwell. "Lead the way, Kermit."

His lips twitched as he ascended the stairs ahead of her, and aimed the laser at the top to illuminate the trip wire. Without disturbing the beam, they stepped over, and started their search of the second floor.

For the next ten minutes, they combed each room, hiding listening devices in one with a beat-up couch and discarded food wrappers, then made their way up to the top floor.

Only two of the six rooms were being used. One had a single mattress, a table with boxes of non-perishable food, two dozen water bottles, and a sleeping bag, pillow, and two new blankets all still in their packaging.

"Nothing's out of place." Matteo nodded toward the mattress. "Looks like they're setting up for company.

Rasheed?

She hoped so, although, it was hard to imagine the smug bastard hiding out in a freezing building.

After scanning what was probably once a coat closet, she opened it to find several new suits, shirts, and shoes. Bella nodded. "Let's cover this room good."

Together they planted two listening devices, along with several cameras in the vents and casings, then she checked the angles on her imager.

"How are they?" Matteo asked, walking to each corner so she could check the visuals.

The cameras were extra important since the room was windowless. It was an inner office, probably a reception area at one time. But, with her imager, and special bullets that cut through walls like butter, she didn't need a window for the kill shot.

Her adrenaline kicked up, and she shivered in anticipation. He was elusive, cunning, heartless. No way did she expect it to go easy. But that was fine with her. She welcomed a challenge. She'd waited a long time for this tango to meet her crosshair.

"We're good," she finally replied. "We need to check the booby-trapped room before they come back."

Using his laser pointer, they avoided the trip wire and entered the final room. Two mattresses flanked the side walls, a cast iron firepit sat in the middle of the room, and a table was set up similar to the other room, with boxes of non-perishable food, another two dozen or so water bottles, except some were open, and a garbage can that sat under the table with discarded wrappers inside.

"This must be where Tariq and Kamal are staying," Matteo said, helping her plant more bugs and cameras. "Do you see any vials or needles or evidence of toxins?"

She shook her head. They'd turned over both mattresses and checked the floorboards. "No. Maybe they only had the one. Or maybe it's on them."

"Go bag." He nodded. "Yeah, I noticed their backpacks, too." And she noticed that this room was also an inner office with no windows. Clever. But not clever enough she thought, as she checked the camera feed and audio. They were going to give up information without knowing it.

"Ash or trash?"

Jerking her head back, she glanced at Matteo. "What?"

"Ash or trash?" he repeated, nodding toward the unlit firepit. "There's evidence here. I can feel it. So, which do you prefer to sift through?"

She felt it too. "Ash," she replied, heading toward the pit.

Last thing she wanted was to encounter used condoms in the trash, although, Bella doubted safe sex was practiced amongst fanatics.

After setting the screened top aside, she removed a pen from her backpack and pushed the ash around, only finding one small shred of burnt paper with part of name or logo visible.

MPSI

She stood and turned to Matteo, smiling at the look of disgust twisting his lips while he squatted to examine the trash he spread out on the floor. "Find anything?"

"Nothing you'd want to see." He shoved everything back in the can, then stood. "How about you?"

Nodding, she moved closer and held up the scrap of paper. "I know I've seen this lettering before." Bella wracked her brain, but she was too distracted. "Here." She used her free hand to dig sanitizer from her bag and squirt some on his palms.

He grinned. "Yeah, you definitely don't want to know what was in there."

"Nope." She shivered and help up a finger. "Keep it to yourself. And the bottle." She dropped it into his palm. "I've got plenty."

For exactly that reason. Her least favorite part of her job.

The grin was still twitching his lips as he shoved it in his pocket and glanced at the burnt scrap. "Let's take that and get out of here before they come back."

With the scrap and pen packed in her backpack, she turned to survey the room again. "There has to be more."

Matteo blew out a breath glanced around. "I agree. Why rig the room to blow if there wasn't evidence to destroy?"

"Exactly." She pointed to the pit. "That's the only thing we didn't move." She pulled out the TI, and double checked her initial sweep of the pit. "Clear."

He grasped the heavy-duty pit and set it aside with ease, as if it were made from aluminum instead of cast iron. "Bingo," he said, pointing to a slight separation in the floor boards.

Bella scanned the area with the TI. "Also clear."

The lack of traps and sensors bespoke of the naiveté of the sympathizers. But it made inspection easier.

Matteo carefully lifted the board, and together they peered inside the cubbyhole to find a stash of weapons, cash, and passports. As quick as possible, they set it on the floor and photographed each piece with her digital camera before returning everything exactly how they'd found it.

"We need to go," Matteo said, setting the pit back in place while she stowed her camera and imager.

Using his laser pointer, they avoided the trip wires and made their way back downstairs. Just as they reached the entrance, the thud of car doors slamming echoed outside.

The men were back.

Chapter Six

With a firm grip, Matteo grabbed her hand and tugged her down the hall into one of the offices as the front door opened and voices echoed inside. The way he pulled her into the adjoining room made Bella smile.

It was cute how he thought she'd never evaded an enemy.

Then he pressed her up against a wall, shielding her body with all those delicious muscles of his, treating her like a helpless victim he needed to protect. Or someone he cared about, her mind whispered. Whatever the reason, it was unnecessary, but damn sweet. And sexy. Actually, hot…the move was very hot. And so was she.

Dammit.

In the space of a few heartbeats, the voices grew fainter, along with footsteps that pounded the stairs…in tandem with her heart.

Fighting the arousal threatening to take over, she pushed Matteo back enough to squirm away. He made her feel too much. And she didn't want to feel. Not now. Not until she finished her mission. The most important one of her life.

"Let's go. It's starting to get dark." Without waiting for his reply, she opened the window and slipped outside, knowing better than to exit through the front door, now that the men were in the building.

Several seconds later, Matteo joined her, and dropped his arm around her shoulders again while they walked down the sidewalk. "I think we should move in together."

With her heart dropping to her feet, Bella stumbled to a halt and twisted to see his expression under the street light. "What?"

His laughter rumbled through her. "You should see your face."

"You're going to see my fist if you don't answer me."

This increased his laughter. "God, I've missed you."

If his words weren't enough to put her into cardiac arrest, the quick kiss to her head nearly did her in. For a guy who used to give her a wide berth, never touched her, and made a point to never be alone with her, he was acting way out of character.

She pulled back a little more and stared at him. Hard. "Who are you and what have you done with Matteo?"

A wicked gleam entered his eyes. "Oh, it's me all right. The version who's starting not to give a shit about rules."

Although she wondered what rules he was referring to, she decided not to ask. Mainly because she liked this version and wanted him to stick around—once she completed her mission. With luck, that would be within the week. "So…you going to tell me about this moving in thing?"

"There's an apartment for rent, right there." He nodded his head toward a building across the street with a sign in one of the second-floor windows. "It has a great view, doesn't it, baby?"

She glanced from it to the one where Tariq and Kamal were, and was admittedly relieved his offer was work-related. Smiling, she leaned into him. "Do you think we can rent it right away, *honeybuns*?"

He snorted. "Looks seedy, so I'm betting cash talks fast." His hold on her shoulder tightened as he led her across the street toward the apartment building.

"Perfect."

It would make breaking back in to search Tariq and Kamal's backpacks for the toxin much easier tonight.

***

Later that evening, Matteo stood next to Bella on the tarmac at the local airport, watching the night sky swallow up the navigation lights of the Learjet with Knight, Brooke, and his father on board. He inhaled then expelled the breath slowly, wishing to God a vial of the toxin was on its way to D.C. with them.

The soft touch of fingers brushing his warmed more than his hand. It warded off the cold chill that threatened over his father's unknown future.

"He'll be okay." Bella laced their fingers together and squeezed. "Knight has the best contacts."

He nodded. "Yeah, the commander never did anything half-assed."

After securing the apartment, Matteo had driven them back to the rehab center, so he could sign the transfer papers and fill Knight in on their findings. He felt confident that Tariq and Kamal were the sympathizers paving the way for Rasheed's arrival, although he'd waited until Bella was out of earshot before sharing that with Knight.

With surveillance in place, and an apartment rented near the rendezvous point, he knew it was only a matter of time before his target made an appearance, and he could make his move — without Bella.

"Let's get back to the apartment." She released his hand to tap his face again. "*Honeybun.*"

He got the impression she liked the feel of his beard. Hell, he'd be more than happy to rub his face over every sweet inch of her delectable body.

He winked. "Whatever you want, baby."

One of the biggest things being a SEAL had taught Matteo was to live in the moment. Not to take anything for granted. Especially time.

Now that they were adults, and it was obvious their chemistry had morphed into the killer range, he was done keeping his distance. To hell with that. Even if she was the one surprisingly fighting it.

Grabbing her hand again, he welcomed the awareness rippling through him, and held tight when she made to tug free. Yeah, they'd definitely reversed their roles, but he was confident he'd win her over after his mission ended.

Provided she didn't find out he was going to protect her father's killer.

His gut hollowed as some of that confidence waned. Surely, she'd understand, once he explained.

"I don't think we're being watched, so you don't have to hold my hand," she said as they walked through the airport parking lot.

"I know," he replied, with a grin that promptly disappeared.

Like his car.

Fuck. "Where the hell's my car?" He released her to glance around the lot. His Charger was missing, and in its place sat a silver Camaro.

"Relax," Bella said, removing a key from her pocket to aim at the sweet ride. The doors unlocked with a muffled thud. "A friend dropped off my car and took yours to fix the window I broke."

He raised his brows. "You know a mechanic that retrieves and delivers cars?"

"Yeah," she said. "Slater can fix anything with wheels. Don't worry, your car is in good hands. I promise. So get in. He also picked up the takeout I ordered, and I know you don't like cold Chinese food."

At the mention of food—and sound of the engine starting—he hurried to her car and climbed into the passenger seat. The delicious aroma of General Tso reminded his stomach he hadn't eaten since lunch. It grumbled in approval. "When the hell did you order all this?"

"The food? Or the cars?" she asked, shifting into drive.

"Both."

"Before we left the rehab center."

In less than ten minutes, they were seated at a table across from each other at the apartment, which she also managed to furnish while they were gone.

The kitchen now sported a brand-new refrigerator. Fully stocked.

He'd checked.

A huge couch, matching armchair, and floor lamp sat in the open-concept living room, along with her backpack, which rested against the wall. Two folding chairs were pushed under a large table in the corner that held state-of-the-art surveillance equipment on top.

Even the bedroom was no longer empty. It housed a damn bed. King size.

He'd checked that, too.

How the hell had she pulled this off?

Using chopsticks, he dug a hunk of chicken out of his container and nodded at the room. "You going to tell me how we acquired this table we're sitting at, and the rest of the furniture in this place?"

She shrugged, and although her lips weren't smiling, amusement sparkled in her eyes. "I know people."

He laughed. "That doesn't sound dangerous or anything."

"Not everyone I know is dangerous."

Somehow, that didn't make him feel any better. In fact, the tightness in his chest increased. He decided to dig a little. "Was it people from work?"

She continued to eat, but gave him another non-committal shrug. Her guard was back up. No sense in pushing. The woman was too stubborn to drop her guard without a fight, and he didn't want to fight.

So he switched gears. "Did your equipment record while we were gone?"

The monitors currently showed Tariq and Kamal reading by the fire in their fire pit, listening to a traditional Middle Eastern folk song that wafted over the speakers to them.

"Yes," she replied. "We can start to comb through it whenever you're ready."

He finished the last of his food, tossed his empty carton in the trash, and smiled at her. "How about now?"

She returned his smile. "Works for me." She threw her trash away and stood. "How about you grab us drinks, and I'll call up the feed?"

"On it." He swiped two bottles of water from the fridge, and joined her at the other table, putting on the headphones she handed him.

For nearly two hours they took turns listening to old feed, while the other monitored the current feed, and glanced through the photos of the stash. They also took turns getting up to survey the building through a set of night vision goggles.

So far, their efforts reaped little reward. But the night was young.

Knight also had a copy of their findings, and Matteo and Bella had already read the files of the men in the passport photos. Tariq and Kamal were Kevin Barber and Ron Preston. Both twenty-four, from upstate New York. No priors. Knight's people were digging further.

Twenty-three minutes into the third hour, he removed the earphones and set them on the table next to Bella's. He glanced around the room, but it was empty. She must be in the bathroom. He hadn't realized she'd gotten up. Probably when he was replaying the argument between the men. Kamal was complaining about Tariq burning the section of the newspaper that listed community events.

Matteo made a mental note to go online and track down the list. But first, he needed to stretch the kink out of his back. The men were asleep on the current feed, their snores competing with one another in a room growing darker as the flames died out in the fire pit.

Rising to his feet, he flexed his shoulders a few times before walking to the window to get his circulation going.

A shadow moving outside the abandoned building snagged his attention. He swiped the night vision goggles off the table and observed the shadow, noting it had very familiar curves.

Bella.

His heart slammed to a halt, before beating at an unnatural rate of speed. "Son-of-a-bitch." Glancing at the wall, he ground out another curse. Her go bag was gone, too. He whipped out his phone to call and chew her out, but he couldn't for two reasons.

One, he couldn't take the chance that it would set off the booby-traps. And two, he didn't have her number.

But she sure as hell had his. Damn woman was going to be the death of him. And the longer he stood watching her slip inside the window they'd exited earlier, and head all the way up to the third floor — in the fucking room where the men now snored — the tighter he grasped the goggles, mirroring the grip apprehension had on his heart.

What the hell was she doing?

They'd already searched the place. Short of going in there to haul her ass out and risk alerting the men, he would have to wait for her to return to chew her out, and get answers, then chew her out some more.

She shouldn't be in there. And she sure as hell shouldn't be in there alone.

For eight minutes and forty-two seconds, he stood helplessly by while she slipped a gas mask over her head and released a silent canister of some kind into their room.

Thank God it wasn't flammable. A few embers still flickered in the pit.

After standing still for a full minute, she made her way to backpacks by their mattresses and riffled through them, pulling out a vial from one. Turning toward the camera, she held it up and he knew she was smiling behind the mask.

He didn't feel like smiling. The invisible weight on his chest rivaled that of a damn building. He could barely breathe, and when he did, it hurt like hell.

Willing her to just grab the damn thing and get out of there, he watched the reckless woman collect a sample of the toxin with a dropper, and place it into another vial. Finally, she put everything back the way she found it, and retraced her steps, making her way out of the building.

All right. She wasn't reckless. In fact, she was capable and efficient, but he still hated her being in that building alone.

Just as relief eased the tightness in his chest, a figure emerged from the shadows. Christ. He wished he had his gun with him, instead of locked in a safe at his dad's place. Her posture remained relaxed and not defensive, so he stayed glued to the spot while she interacted with the figure before it disappeared into the night, and she crept toward the apartment.

Once he was certain she was in the building, he set the goggles on the table and started to pace, trying to work off the adrenaline and anger heating his veins. He was going to wring her pretty little neck.

By the time she entered and set her pack on the floor, he hadn't calmed down. In fact, he was close to losing his shit. Which explained why he pounced on her, grasping her by the shoulders and pressing her against the wall. "Are you crazy?"

With a strength that startled him, she immediately reversed their positions, until she slammed him against the wall and glared into his face. "I could ask you the same thing."

For several seconds, they took turns as *presser*, until he used his body to keep her in place, his ragged breaths mixing with hers.

Big mistake.

All the adrenaline pounding through his veins switched to a desire so fierce he throbbed. She did too, in the form of a tremor he absorbed with his body. He'd never been so damn turned on in his life.

Her gaze darkened to a deep emerald as she stared at his mouth. Not enough training in the world could prevent him from reacting to the need coursing between them — to prevent him from breaking the promise he made to his dad to treat her like a sister, all those years ago. His temperature spiked to unsafe and his mind shut down.

Fuck it.

Releasing his grip on her shoulders, he eased back just enough to cup her face in both hands and brush his thumb over her parted lips.

The time for denial was over. It was time to taste the woman he'd longed to kiss for more than a decade.

Chapter Seven

With his heart slamming against his ribs, and need spiraling out of control, he lowered his mouth until they shared a heated breath.

Then his phone rang.

Followed by hers.

"Shit," someone said.

Probably him. Could've been her.

Either way, they broke apart to answer their calls.

The only reason he let go of his desire to kiss Bella was because Knight was supposed to update him on his father. Pulling the phone out of his pocket, he drew in a deep breath, then released it as he noted Knight's number on his caller ID.

"How's my father, sir?"

"Good, but he'll be even better now that the doctors can identify the toxin, thanks to the sample that's on its way."

How the fuck...?

He shot his gaze to Bella, but her back was to him as she talked on her phone.

The figure in the shadows must've been one of Knight's agents.

"Latest chatter still puts Rasheed in Atlantic City this month. But all indications are he hasn't surfaced yet."

"Well, Tariq and Kamal are definitely waiting for someone to arrive." He went on to explain the room with the bed, and clothes, and food.

"Yeah, they're expecting company."

"Have your people gotten anything off the photos of the contents of their stash and trash we sent?" he asked, noting that Bella was off the phone. "Hang on, sir. I'm going to put you on speaker, so Bella can hear too." He hit the button and walked toward her with the phone in his palm. "Go ahead, sir."

"Hi, Bella," the commander greeted. "Brooke and I will be flying back up in the morning to assist. I already sent both of you the files on the guys you're surveilling. Did you get them?"

She smiled as she neared. "Hello, sir, and yes, we've already read them."

"Good. Our technicians determined the weapons came from a shop in Camden."

Matteo bit back a curse. It was way too easy. "I don't like it. They didn't even try to scratch out the serial numbers. They're either really reckless, or following orders, which would be worse."

"I know." The commander's sigh rustled through the phone. "It's the reckless part that has me worried. By not covering their tracks, it tells me they don't plan to get caught."

"They plan to get dead," Bella said.

He nodded. "Exactly."

"It backs up the chatter we've heard about an attack during the holidays," Knight said. "Is there anything big going on in AC this month?"

"A few things," Bella replied. "A live, televised Christmas concert at the Capris, with several popular singers. A Christmas parade down the boardwalk. Each casino hosts huge New Year's Eve bashes. And my personal favorite, a Grinch convention where I think Matteo would fit right in, since he loves the holiday so much."

The commander laughed. "You're right. Reaper always did channel an inner Grinch this time of the year."

"Reaper?" Her head snapped back, and eyes lit with interest. "That's your SEAL handle?"

He cocked his head. "Yes."

"I gave it to him myself," Knight said, a measure of pride in his tone. "His aim was unmatched, and unlike the song, enemies did fear him."

She narrowed her eyes, then nodded. "Suits you."

Unsure if it was a compliment or not, he decided to take it as one and nodded back, before changing the subject. "Kamal had complained about Tariq burning the section of the newspaper that had listed community events. I'm betting there was something of interest on that list."

"Any evidence of it in the ash?" Knight asked.

"No." Bella shook her head. "The only thing bigger than ash was the piece of paper I photographed and sent you with the letters MPSI on it."

"Our technician ran it through his computers, and cross-referenced with your local businesses and letterhead and found a match to Simpson Enterprises. Alan Simpson is a bigwig from the big apple who owns the Capris with a silent partner from the west coast."

Bella's chin lifted. "Every year he throws a large holiday party for his office employees and all the dealers at his shore house, just up the road in Brigantine. And by house, I mean huge, sprawling mansion."

"When is it?" Knight asked.

"This Friday." Bella grinned. "Two days from now."

"Good. That'll give my guy time to hack into security, so Brooke can be your eyes when you take Matteo as your date and copy Simpson's hard drives."

She blinked. "I'm more than capable of doing that on my own."

"You're not going alone," Matteo ground out, as all the anxiety and emotion from the past hour came crashing back.

"He's right, Bella," Knight chimed in. "If Simpson is involved with terrorists, he has the money and the power to back something big."

"And to be a real threat," he added, refusing to let her go without him.

She blew out a breath. "Fine. He probably has more than one computer, anyhow."

"Get some rest," Knight said. "Things are going to heat up."

Matteo barely held back a snort. Truer words. His gaze met Bella's, but the hunger and need were gone, replaced by a closed calm.

Her walls were back up. "Will do."

"See you tomorrow," Knight said, before the line went dead.

"Do you want the couch or the bed?" she asked, arms folded across her chest in a classic ward-off stance.

"Couch," he replied, ignoring the "warding". "But we need to talk."

Her gaze slowly narrowed. "About what?"

"Are you kidding?" He reeled back. "About the fact you snuck out of here and into the damn building without me. What the hell were you thinking?"

She unfolded her arms to jam her hands on her hips. "I hate to break it to you, frogman, but I am more than capable of performing a snatch n' grab on my own."

"That's not the point."

"No?" Her chin lifted. "Then what is?"

"I don't want you getting hurt because of me."

Her posture relaxed and some of the fight disappeared from her stance. "I'd do just about anything for you, but don't think for one minute that what I did tonight was strictly for you. I did it for me, too. He may be your father, but he's my godfather—my second father. So, I did it for me too."

He should've realized that, but unexpectedly running into her today had fucked up his brain. He nodded. "Thanks, by the way."

A smile tugged her lips. "No need. We're like family, right?"

Not like she thought. Never like that. But that was an argument for another time. "Look, I just want you to know you don't have to go it on your own. Not while I'm around."

She cocked her head as the warmth faded from her gaze. "Yeah, well, you haven't been around, Matteo. You took off. Married the Navy, and left me behind. So I've learned to improvise."

Ouch.

He scrubbed a hand over his face. "Look, Bella…"

"No. Don't." She held up a hand and shook her head. "You don't get to say anything, just because it suits you now. Forget it. I'm going to bed."

Swiping her backpack off the floor, she strode into the bedroom and shut the door. The ominous sound of the lock clicking in place was a blatant emphasis that this time, she was putting up the barriers, closing doors — shutting him out of her life.

But it wasn't going to work.

He was a SEAL, and known for his persistence. He'd already made up his mind to break the promise to his dad, and once Matteo made up his mind, he didn't turn back. It was a waste of time and energy. Both precious.

Something he came to realize when his mother dropped dead from a massive heart attack while putting up Christmas decorations five years ago. Another reason to hate the holidays. The anniversary of her death was fast approaching. Hopefully, this mission would keep him too damn busy to dwell on it.

He'd rather think about Bella, and how much fun it was going to be to break through her walls and put their chemistry to the test.

***

By the time Friday evening approached, Bella was ready to get on with the mission. The more time she spent around Matteo, the more cracks appeared in the wall around her heart, giving her old feelings a chance to surface.

Sure, it'd be amazing for a while. But she knew how it would all end. She wasn't stupid. He was a SEAL, and he'd return to the teams, once his father recovered. And Angelo Santarelli was too stubborn not to.

So, once again, Matteo would leave her on the beach with her heart exposed and bleeding while he disappeared into the sunset.

She couldn't go through that again.

Refused to go through it again.

With luck, tonight would be the night to put things right. She had a good feeling about it. There was something on Simpson's computers to point her in Rasheed's direction, and that meant she could complete her actual mission.

Hanging out with Knight and Brooke was fine—fun even—but at the end of the day, Bella answered to a different boss. Her phone call with the General this morning, reaffirmed her focus.

Find and neutralize Rasheed.

Lord knew she'd love nothing more.

Okay, there were a few other things, but they all involved Matteo. Naked. And she'd already decided that was a bad idea, and moved on.

Mostly.

Dammit. Awareness fluttered through her belly.

Waste of time.

Standing in front of the full-length mirror in her bedroom at home, she smoothed her hands over her hips and studied her reflection. The red dress was festive, yet sexy, with thin straps, a plunging neckline, and a right leg slit from hem to thigh.

Brooke walked into the room, her dark brown ponytail swinging as she stopped dead and whistled. "You trying to give Matteo a heart attack? Or make him eat his heart out by showing him what he passed up?"

The astute woman was the only one who knew her history with Matteo. Or lack of one. "Something like that."

"Well, this dress will do it." Brooke nodded. "Might I suggest you only pull some of your hair up, so it exposes just enough neck to tantalize?"

Bella smiled. "Ooh, you're good." She quickly pinned up the sides, tugged a few pieces loose to soften the look, then paused to wonder what in the world she was doing.

This wasn't a date. It was a mini mission to copy hard drives, not tease Matteo. She straightened her shoulders and lifted her chin.

To hell with it. She could do both.

Adding the diamond necklace and earring set her father had given her mother at Christmas, a week before his death, Bella embraced the sense of retribution nearly at hand.

"Tell me you have some do-me heels?" Brooke's gaze met hers in the mirror.

She grinned and opened her closet. "Several."

Never had their friendship made more sense. Except for that time they took out a pair of Russian mobsters, using knives they both concealed strapped to their thighs.

Tonight, Bella wore one on her left leg.

"Perfect." Brooke rubbed her hands together in a rare show of emotion. "Those. Definitely." Her friend pointed to a pair of black stilettos with diamond encrusted straps. "They go with your necklace."

Bella sat on the bed to slip into the heels, and had just finished buckling the straps when a knock sounded on the front door. Her heart rocked, and stomach fluttered. Which was foolish, because this wasn't an actual date.

"I'll get it," Brooke said, disappearing out the door before Bella could blink.

Or get up. She was still sitting on the bed. Which was probably a good thing, since her legs were unusually shaky.

Which was bullshit.

Daring her legs to buckle, she rose to her feet, straightened her spine, and walked out to greet Matteo.

Chapter Eight

Since their full-body contact wrestling match against the apartment wall the other night, Bella appeared to go through pains not to be alone with him. Matteo recognized the play. Hell, he'd mastered it during his youth, in order to resist her lure.

But, unlike the youthful Bella, Matteo gave her the space she sought. Knight and Brooke took over the surveillance at the apartment, which left the two of them free to go back to their houses, and regular routines. He continued to work at the pizza shop, making it a point to chat up more of the locals, and local store owners. Some were nice. Other's leery, while two were downright rude.

According to Omar, the brother and sister duo were French-Canadian, and won no popularity contest amongst the other shop owners. And even though they wanted top dollar for their rugs, and silk scarves, jewelry, and pottery from around the world, they managed to stay in business for almost three years now.

That put them on the top of his list of possible importers of the human kind. In case the Simpson thing was a bust tonight.

Was it bad that he suddenly couldn't wait to get to the study? Not because of the hard drives they needed to download, but because of the stunning woman who'd just walked into her living room and sucked all the air from his lungs.

Holy shit. She looked amazing.

But...where the hell was the rest of her dress?

Breaking out in a sweat, he tugged at his collar in an attempt to cool off. His tongue swelled two sizes too big for his mouth. He had no idea how to fix it. And his dick? He'd never experienced an instant hard-on...until now. Bella always stirred something in him. Made him hard, with a look or a smile. But this? It went beyond.

Felt like he had a damn anchor attached to his groin.

And yeah, he had a very good idea how to remedy the situation, but now was not the time.

"Hi, Matteo," she said, in a voice as soft as the smooth skin she bared for all to see. At least, he imagined it felt soft. Silky soft. "You clean up nice."

Nice? He didn't feel nice. Heat, anger, arousal, all three coursed through his body, making him nuts. He wanted to cover her up, and strip her naked at the same time. Fierce need fluctuated between protecting her and burying himself balls-deep inside her gorgeous curves.

That was neither clean, nor nice. But he'd bet his last breath it would be life-altering.

How the hell was he supposed to carry out a mission when all he could think about was touching Bella?

As she swayed closer, flashing an exquisite mile-long leg, every throbbing inch of him was aware of every sweet inch of her. His fingers tightened around the rose in his grasp, as he fought the urge to run his hands up her arms to see if her skin really was as soft as it appeared.

"You take my breath, Bella." The fact he'd spoken the words out loud proved it, because the lack of oxygen to the brain must be the reason behind his loose lips.

"I—uh—thank you," she said, color rising into her cheeks.

He hadn't seen her blush since she was in middle school. It looked amazing on her.

Remembering the flower in his hand, he gave her the single rose, no longer long-stemmed, since he'd gripped the sucker so hard it snapped in half. "For you. Or…at least, what's left of it."

She grinned, and when their fingers brushed her blush increased. "Thank you. But you didn't have to." Turning, she walked to the adjoining kitchen, filled a glass with water, and dropped the rose inside. "I mean, it's not a real date or anything," she added, before tossing the broken half in the trash.

He could relate. That wouldn't do.

Moving toward Bella, Matteo ignored the fact Brooke was watching, and leaned against the counter. "Why not?"

Her back stiffened, and she turned to face him. "Why not…what?"

"Why can't this be a real date?" Then a thought occurred, and it was his turn to stiffen. "Are you already seeing someone?"

"What?" she asked again, then frowned and shook her head. "No. Like you, I'm married to my job."

A wry smile pulled his lips. "I just got separated, remember?" That should've hurt like hell, but at the moment, it barely caused a ripple.

Probably because he was in the middle of a mission.

"Doesn't mean it's okay to use me as a substitute." She pushed past to walk back in the other room.

He reached out to grasp her arm, and waited until she met his gaze. "I'd never use you, Bella. Never have in the past, won't do it now, or in the future."

And…damn…he knew it. Her skin *was* soft. He loosened his hold to lightly brush his thumb up and down her arm before releasing her.

She rubbed her arm where he'd touched her. "You can't predict the future, Matteo. No one can. Unless you're Madame Salome, three shops down from yours."

Although he wanted Bella to acknowledge that he'd never use her, he went along with her attempt to lighten the mood. "I hear she gives five percent off on Tuesdays."

Some of the tightness eased from her shoulders. "I just want to go to the party and get the hard drives copied."

"And we will," he said, unable to let go of the idea now that it had formed. "But since it is a party, and we're supposed to pretend to be on a date, why not treat it like one and have fun doing it?" He glanced at the silent Brooke. "Am I right?"

The woman held up her hands and shook her head. "Oh, no. Don't draw me into this. I'm just here to pass out your earpieces, and to park three miles from Simpson's so I can monitor security and walk you through any obstacles, while Knight holds down the fort, aka, apartment."

"Right." Bella nodded. "So, you see? There's no room for fun, or fake dates, or real ones."

"I didn't say that, either." Brooke shrugged, slight tug to her lips. "I just said to leave me out of it. What the two of you choose to do about your killer chemistry is your own business."

She dug inside her go bag and stepped close to drop a miniscule silver disk into each of their hands, along with a bigger cylinder with a key ring attached.

"That's it?" He blinked at the little bug. "Won't it get stuck in the ear?"

Bella shook her head. "It feels weird at first, like it's going to get stuck, but it never does. You put it in like this." She dropped it in her ear and it disappeared.

He leaned close. "Is it stuck?"

She smiled. "No. It's just small and nearly impossible for others to see. Which is the name of the game."

"How do you get it out?" He didn't relish going to the ER to have them fish a listening device from his ear.

"With this magnet." Again, Bella demonstrated, sticking the bigger cylinder near her ear and the bug practically flew out, making a loud smacking noise as it stuck to the magnet. "You try."

He dropped the bug in his ear, surprised at how light it felt. A few shakes of his head didn't dislodge it. Impressed, he held the magnet close, and just as it had for Bella, the bug zipped out to stick to the magnet. "Is it just audio?"

Brooke spoke up, placing the go bag back on her shoulder. "No, it also picks up speech. Plus, it's a transmitter, and tracking device."

"Clever," he said, dropping it back into his ear, then added the magnet to his key ring so it too, would go undetected, should he be searched. "Time to go."

"Do you need to take an invitation or something?" Brooke asked as Bella put the device back in her ear, and magnet on a key ring she shoved in her small purse.

"Yes. I have it in here." She tapped her purse on her way to the closet by the door where she removed a long coat.

Matteo took it from her and held it open. "Allow me."

For a split second, her gaze flashed, and he thought she was going to give him shit, but instead, she thanked him and turned around to slip her arms in the sleeves. Never one to look a gift horse in the mouth, he smoothed the coat over her shoulders and inhaled that unique, sweet and spicy perfume of hers.

A calm settled over Matteo. At ease, he opened the door, and waited for the women to leave before following them outside. It was a beautiful night, with little wind, which was rare so close to the water. Falling into step alongside Bella, he automatically cupped her elbow, in case she tripped in those sexy damn heels that made his dick twitch.

Brooke headed for her car in Bella's driveway. "I'll turn on the surveillance equipment to make sure your earpieces are working."

He nodded, but kept his hand on Bella's elbow on their way to his driveway next door. If he had known she was going to wear stilts on her feet, he would've parked in her driveway, even though there was only fifty feet of side yard between the houses.

With each step she took, he cringed inwardly, expecting her to break her ankle, especially on the sand and grass that separated their driveways.

But she moved with a confident grace that turned out to be sexier than those damn shoes.

Drawing in the cool night air, he listened to the sound of the ocean rolling in behind their houses, assaulting the beach with a relentless caress. An amazing force of nature.

Like the woman by his side.

Letting her go, he opened the door and thought about her unwillingness to call tonight a date. In truth, she was right. It was work.

Possibly dangerous work, which was the reason his Glock was safely tucked inside his ankle holster.

Bella was with him.

And, although he was slowly coming around to accepting the fact she was an agent of some sort, a very capable one, he would never lose his desire to protect her.

Not happening. Ever.

"Thank you," she said, slipping into her seat.

He waited until she was settled before shutting the door and heading to the driver's side. Adrenaline started to kick up. He inhaled several deep breaths and got in.

"Testing," Brooke said, her voice surprisingly loud through the tiny device in his ear. "Can you hear me, Bella?"

"Roger," Bella answered next to him. "Loud and clear."

"And you, Reaper?"

A smile tugged his lips. It was damn good to put that handle to use again. "Roger. Loud and clear," he replied, too.

"Ditto," Brooke said. "Let's roll."

The mansion was a twelve-minute drive from his house. Matteo knew, because he'd clocked it the day before when he'd done a little recon. Simpson's place was more like a mini fortress, with high walls, and state of the art

125

security. But Knight had insisted his hacker could get in, and link Brooke to the system. He trusted them both, but wished the op fell to just him. How or why Bella was involved, he couldn't remember. It would be better if she wasn't.

For several reasons. First and foremost, her safety. Second, he was slightly worried there might be blatant evidence about Rasheed on the computers that Bella could see straight away.

Instinct told him it was best to keep any knowledge of Rasheed from her. He knew he might have to lie to her, but he would if it meant saving lives.

Didn't mean he'd like it, though.

"You're awfully quiet," she said, gaining his attention. "You okay?"

He pushed his misgivings aside and smiled. "Of course. You?"

"Peachy."

His smile grew. "I'd guess more of a juicy Granny Smith apple."

"Ah. Sweet with a bit of tang." She nodded.

"Exactly."

"And I would guess you were a prune."

He reeled back. "What?" A fucking prune? Soft laughter sounded in his ear, reminding him their conversations were no longer private tonight. "Why a prune?"

"Because, you start out delicious, and even subjected to harshness, you persevere, reinvent yourself, get rid of the superfluous, until only the best remains."

Put like that, it was a high compliment, and the unexpectedness of it shocked him the most. He cleared his throat, truly at a loss as to how to respond.

Christ, if the guys could see him now. Tongue-tied because a beautiful woman compared him to a fruit that cleans out your system.

"Thanks," he finally said. "I thought you were going to go the laxative route."

She snickered. "Well, there are times when you're full of shit."

"There is that." He laughed because it was true.

Brooke burst out laughing in his ear. "Oh, my God. You two are too funny."

That's when it dawned on him. Their whole damn prune conversation was recorded. He swallowed a curse and changed the subject. "So, is there anything I should know about this Simpson guy and his parties?"

Bella sobered and shook her head. "I've seen him walking through the casino, but never met him."

"Were you at last year's party?" he asked, as he drove over the bridge that connected Atlantic City to Brigantine.

"Yes, but I also studied the layout Knight sent yesterday."

"So did I." Before recon.

"Then tonight should be a piece of cake," she said, but he didn't feel as confident.

When he and his brothers were given a mission, they'd devised a plan, then practiced the hell out of it until every move became second nature. He and Bella hadn't practiced a damn thing together.

Kind of hard when she kept her distance.

"All right. I'm going to hang back here and set up surveillance," Brooke said. "But if you need backup, just say the code word *taffy*, and I'll have your six."

"Roger," he replied.

Bella snickered. "Matteo has a soft spot for taffy."

"Is that right?" Amusement lightened Brooke's tone.

"Yeah. Vanilla." Bella smirked.

"I'll keep it in mind should I ever need to bribe the Reaper," Brooke said, smile still evident in her tone.

He chuckled. "You do that. I prefer the shorter over the longer, but I'd never turn any down."

"How many boxes have you been through since you returned?" Bella asked.

Damn woman knew him too well. "Three." He slowed down as they neared the property. "Dig out the invitation. It's showtime."

As they waited two deep in line at the security gate, he used the time to note only two guards at the gate, one on the second-floor balcony, and another at the north side of the mansion. Not a lot of security. He hoped they weren't all inside.

By the time they entered, checked Bella's coat, and mingled with the others while pretending to enjoy the free-flowing flutes of champagne, Matteo pegged eight more security.

"Nine," he corrected with a grin, holding his flute up to a young couple waving from across the room. He recognized them from the shop. In fact, he recognized quite a few customers.

"And my feed puts another four upstairs," Brooke said. "Seventeen. Not an excessive total, considering the number of guests tonight exceeds one-fifty."

True. If Simpson was involved in something, Matteo didn't get any vibes it was happening tonight. The mood was as festive as the lights and decorations adorning the walls, staircase, and tall Christmas trees scattered throughout the first floor. The atmosphere was bright and flashy and as commercialized at the holidays.

January couldn't get here soon enough.

"Do you have a visual on Simpson yet?" Brooke asked.

"No." Bella sipped her drink and walked around with her arm through his. "But he'll show. He likes to address the crowd and talk a good game. Which will be our best time to hit the office, because the crowd will gather near in the foyer as he talks from the balcony."

Matteo wished Bella had accepted his invitation to come over last night for supper, so they could've discussed all this. He preferred to plan, not improvise. But, he did enjoy a challenge. "The guards will be busy with the crowd."

She nodded. "We'll be busy, too."

"Starting now." He took her flute and set it on a nearby credenza. "Let's dance."

Not giving her a chance to refuse, Matteo tugged Bella to the makeshift dance floor on the other side of the entrance, and pulled her into his arms. Surprisingly, *Ms. Rebellious* didn't argue. In fact, she slid her arms around his neck and melted against him with a sweet sigh that shivered over his neck.

Damn. Already on high alert with adrenaline, his body welcomed the friction of her soft curves pressing close while they slowly swayed to the music. He'd never felt so alive. It was crazy. Every brush, every sway, increased the heat and awareness running rampant through him.

But of course, he could never seem to catch a break with Bella.

The music ended, and Alan Simpson chose that fucking moment to appear on the balcony above. Swallowing disappointment down with a silent oath, he reluctantly released Bella, who blinked away the daze from her gaze.

"As Reaper said before, it's showtime," Brooke announced in their ears. "I've just looped the feed in the hall and office, and unlocked the office door. You're good to go."

He grabbed Bella's hand and pushed through the gathering guests in the pretense of wanting to get closer to hear their host. Stopping at the outskirts, he waited until security moved with the crowd, before slipping behind them down the hall and into the office.

Following Bella inside, he closed the door. "How does it look out there, Brooke? Anyone notice?"

"Nope. All clear. Carry on."

Bella already had her purse on the desk and the thumb drives in the laptop and desktop. "You're sure security isn't going to be alerted when I turned these on?"

"Yes," Brooke replied. "Don't let the tiny size fool you. The device is more than a thumb drive. It's some funky mojo magic thingy."

Matteo smiled. Now he knew why Bella and Brooke got on so well. They were both more tactical than technical.

"Okay. Booting," Bella announced. "How's the hall?"

"Clear. Trust me, I'll tell you if it's not," Brooke stated. "And the actual security feed in the office is looped to show an empty office."

"And the speech?" He walked past a plush couch to the filing cabinet on the other side. Surprise washed through him when he tugged the top drawer opened with ease.

"Still going strong," Brooke replied.

The next two drawers opened as well, but when Matteo tried the bottom one, it didn't budge. "Bingo."

"Here." Bella stopped rifling through the desk to hand him two hair pins from her hair.

"Thanks." He used them to pick the lock and open the drawer, before giving them back.

At quick glance, nothing looked different than the other three drawers, but it had been locked for a reason. He snapped photos of all the name tabs, then removed the first few files to photograph the contents, when he spotted a manila envelope at the bottom of the drawer.

His pulse quickened as he opened the flap and pulled out a passport and NJ driver's license for one very bald, clean-cut middle-aged man name Robert Zimmerman. But Matteo recognized the bastard, even without his hair and full beard.

Rasheed Al-Zahawi.

With one eye on Bella, he quickly utilized the app Knight had loaded onto his phone to send the photos he took straight to a mainframe, instead of storing them on his phone. When he finished, he returned the IDs where he found them, then opened the files he'd removed earlier and photographed their contents.

Again, nothing looked amiss, but he was hopeful Knight and his people would scour every line of every photo and find a damn clue to the time and method of Rasheed's arrival.

"Bella, how's it going?" Brooke asked.

"Desktop is almost done. Laptop is at eighty-seven percent," she answered.

"Matteo, you almost done with that drawer?"

He pulled out the last few files and nodded. "Yeah."

If Brooke had noticed him with the IDs, the woman wisely remained silent. Matteo hated keeping secrets from Bella, but he didn't want her messing with terrorists on her own. That's exactly what she would do, too. Her little stunt the other night with Tariq and Kamal proved it.

"Good, because the speech just ended," Brooke informed. "Finish up and get out of there."

After snapping the last couple of photos, he shoved the files back, closed the drawer, then tugged to make sure it locked. "Done."

Straightening, he pocketed his phone and turned to find Bella powering down the laptop and shoving the tiny flash drive inside some kind of special compartment camouflaged in the sequins on her dress.

She returned the laptop back to the corner of the desk and glanced at the other computer. "Desktop is at ninety-five percent," she announced. "Ninety-six."

"Pull it," Brooke ordered. "Security is doing a sweep of the rooms in the hall."

Bella shook her head. "No. I'll get it. Just need another minute."

He stepped close, adrenaline kicking into overdrive. "It takes nearly that long to power down."

"Two doors away."

Matteo glanced around, looking for another exit, but there were no windows. Just the one door.

"Ninety-nine." Bella smiled. "One hundred."

"They're next door," Brooke informed.

While he shut down the computer, Bella stashed the flash drive with the other in her dress, then pulled the pins from one side of her hair and ran her fingers through the brown waves. Keeping calm, he rounded the corner of the desk and met her in front.

"They're back in the hall, heading your way," Brooke updated them.

Shit. He went to push Bella behind him, but she stood firm.

"Unbutton your shirt," she told him.

"What?" His heart rocked. Must've heard her wrong.

Pushing the strap down on her dress, she blew out an impatient breath. "Never mind."

A second later, she grasped his shirt and ripped it open. Buttons were still flying in the air as she pulled him down on top of her on the couch.

Then kissed him.

"Incoming in five…four…"

Matteo knew it. As sure as the blood pumping through his veins, he never doubted Bella was the one who ruled his heartbeat. Owned his soul. Made him whole. She was it for him, and just the briefest brush of her lips on his solidified everything. Confirmed what he'd known for years. She was the one.

She was home.

Hungry and eager, her mouth moved under his, demanding, giving, driving all thought, all worry—everything from his mind, until only need remained.

Now that his mouth was on hers, nothing and no one was going to stop him from kissing the woman he'd desired for years. Moaning, she shifted under him, while her fingers…damn…her wicked fingers stroked his abs, sending a shaft of heat down his spine.

So good.

Cupping her head with one hand, he ran the other down the supple leg she wrapped around his hip, and deepened the kiss, sweeping his tongue inside her hot mouth, tasting, exploring, acquainting himself with her very essence. Her forbidden essence. The one he'd denied himself for more than a decade.

Exquisite.

The sound of a door creaking barely registered in his fogged brain.

"Hey! You shouldn't be in here."

But the hard tone penetrated, along with several snickers. Bella stiffened underneath him, and Matteo was secretly pleased he wasn't the only one who'd momentarily forgotten about their mission.

Hell, he'd forgotten everything once her lips brushed his…including to breathe.

Drawing back, he inhaled and blinked in an attempt to bring the room back into focus. Christ. He knew kissing Bella was going to rock his world, he just hadn't expected their first kiss to be recorded, or witnessed by a roomful of smirking thugs.

"What are you two doing in here?" The only non-smirking thug glowered down at them.

Using his dazed state to help them out, Matteo let his body take its time to switch into SEAL mode as he rolled off her and pulled them both to their feet. He did, however, keep Bella behind him, using his body to shield her from their view.

Damn woman stepped next to him.

"I...ah...think that was probably obvious," she said, pulling the strap onto her shoulder before smoothing down her dress.

With a blush flooding her face and grin tugging her lips, she managed to appear both wicked and innocent at the same time. Enthralled, the thugs licked their lips and gawked at her. Unfamiliar, primal urges rampaged through Matteo, and although he knew it helped their predicament to have the guards off-balance, no way would he stand there and let them fuck her with their eyes.

Grinding his teeth, he curled his hands into fists, the muscles in his arms bunching under the pressure as he stepped forward.

Chapter Nine

The air around Bella heated and crackled, and she knew without glancing at Matteo that the big, bad SEAL was about to pounce on the three men she was deliberately trying to entice so they could get the hell out of dodge.

Reaching for his hand, she found it curled into a tight fist that shook. Not good. Normally, any man who had issues with other men looking at her, or talking to her, received a one-way boot to the curb. But this wasn't just any man. It was Matteo. The only man she ever wanted to be with, to give everything to and take everything in return. He was once her world. The exception to everything and exceptional above all others.

So, of course this possessiveness was an unexpected turn on.

Some strange, warm, crazy emotion fluttered through her chest. For Matteo to be riled enough to blow their covers, and chance failing his mission, it meant one of two things. He was either stupid, or motivated by his deep feelings for her.

Matteo Santarelli was far from stupid.

Both terrified and thrilled by that knowledge, Bella stroked his hand to loosen his fist and entwined their fingers. "We were just looking for somewhere private," she told the guards. "Isn't that right, honey?" She left off the "buns" part.

Barely.

When he didn't respond, and his attention remained on the guards, she squeezed his hand and swayed closer to brush against his arm. He blinked and glanced at her, his gaze softening with a smile. "That's right, babe. I can never seem to get enough of you." He released her hand to slip his arm around her shoulders and draw her into his side as his attention returned to the guards again. "Sorry, fellas. We just wanted a little bit of alone time and this was the only door unlocked."

The men immediately frowned.

"Every door in this hall was locked," one said.

Bella shook her head. "Not this one. How else did we get in?"

"How indeed?" Another narrowed his gaze. The one in charge. "If you're telling the truth, you won't mind if I check your purse." He grabbed it from the desk where she'd tossed it earlier.

Matteo stiffened. "Wait just a minute."

She played along, patting his arm—at least, she assumed he was acting. "It's okay. They have a right to be concerned."

The guy dumped the contents of her purse out on the desk, but of course he found nothing. The idiot didn't even bother to look at her ID before shoving her stuff back inside and handing her the purse. While he did all that, the other two guards checked drawers and the computers, and they each met the gaze of the man in charge and shook their heads.

He removed the radio from his belt and spoke into it, "Slight situation in the office."

"Seriously?" Brooke muttered in her earpiece. "The men just motioned there was nothing wrong."

True. She held her breath to see if they were going to get Simpson involved. Hopefully, not. The last thing they wanted was a face-to-face with the man abetting a terrorist...before the terrorist made an appearance.

"Check the feed," the guard in charge ordered.

Bella silently echoed Brooke's sigh of relief.

"Negatory. Feeds been jacked up all night," came the reply. "Trouble with the locks, too. Reports of guests in some of the rooms."

"See?" She lifted a shoulder and smiled. "Sounds like we weren't the only ones making merry."

His gaze narrowed again. "Maybe, but we're still going to have to search you before we let you leave." He clipped the radio back on his belt and moved closer.

Matteo immediately stepped in front of her. "Like hell," he ground out, hands curling into fists again. "If you have a problem with us being in this room call the police. But you are not touching her."

"Damn," Brooke muttered in her earpiece.

Bella agreed. The outrage and warning in his tone matched his stony profile and fit with their covers, but she knew not one word of that was acting. Matteo had switched from SEAL on a mission to SEAL protecting his woman.

His woman…

She wasn't sure when that had happened. Hell, for years Bella had tried to get him to see her in that light. Get him to let her in. Instead, he'd cut her out of his life. Now, he was back in it a couple days, kissed her once, and all of a sudden, she was his woman?

A thrill like none she'd ever known raced through her, warming her up from the inside out. She squashed it down. Hard.

Not how it worked.

At least, not with her. No matter how damn amazing that kiss was, knocking her on her ass—even though she'd already been in that position. His touch, his taste, it tipped her world on its axis. The kiss was much better than she'd ever imagined. Better than her fantasies. Mind altering, but it didn't make up for the fact she'd opened up to him and he'd turned her down cold, then left. For over a decade. The only time they'd crossed paths was at his mother's funeral—five years ago tomorrow.

"No need to call the police," one of the other guards said, jerking her back to the present. "You two can go back and enjoy the party."

Some of the stiffness eased from Matteo's shoulders. He nodded, then grabbed her hand. "Come on, baby. Let's get out of here."

She smiled as they walked to the door one of the guards opened. "Yeah. I think there's some mistletoe out there with your name on it. I know how much you love Christmas."

His lips twitched as they walked into the hall. "That part for sure, if you're involved."

"They're still watching you," Brooke told them. "You'd better kiss again, so they don't suspect."

No one was visible from where Bella stood, but her friend did have a better view.

"Gladly," Matteo said, stopping to press her against the wall, his gaze dialed to smoldering as his mouth took hers in a hot, demanding kiss she happily returned...for the mission.

Not because she wanted it more than air. Or because he kissed with a deep hunger and absolute thoroughness unmatched by any other. No. It was for the mission. To keep up appearances. To taste his hunger and bask in the knowledge that she was the one he wanted. The one he was kissing like he couldn't get enough.

The feeling was mutual. And just like before, a warm fuzziness invaded her brain, manifesting to swallow all thoughts, the mission, her surroundings, until her focus narrowed to only them.

His beard tantalized and teased, while his mouth plundered and possessed, giving her all that she demanded and more. Running her palms up his chest, she moaned at the feel of hot, hard flesh bared beneath his open shirt— because the buttons lay scattered all over the office floor.

"Okay, guys. I think they got the idea." Brooke's voice startled them to a stop. "I'm surprised you didn't set off the sprinklers. Damn. I need a cold shower."

Matteo released her mouth and set his forehead to hers, muttering something about the ocean. She couldn't be sure, though. Damn man stole her breath and fogged her brain.

Panting, she worked to clear her mind and regain control of her body that annoyingly lacked strength. Mainly in her legs.

What the hell? No man had ever physically drained her before.

This wasn't good. She needed her strength. Her job wasn't doable without it. And her job was her life. Once upon a time, Matteo had filled that role. She would've given anything to be in his arms like this, clutching his shirt, sharing a breath, awareness trembling through her heated body. But she wasn't the same girl she'd been back then.

Oh, she still wanted him with her last breath, that would never change. Not in a million years. But if he knew how she lived her life, the things she'd done in the name of justice, it was doubtful he'd still want her. Or even like her.

The last part she feared the most.

It was the reason she couldn't pursue their attraction.

With that fear prevalent in her mind, she patted his chest and forced a smile to her lips. "We should go before they change their minds."

Or before she changed hers, about pursuing.

***

For the following eight hours, Matteo tried to concentrate on figuring out how Simpson planned to smuggle Rasheed into the country, but his mind kept returning to Bella and her hot kisses, amazing taste, and the way she responded to him with an eagerness he'd never experienced, or would ever forget.

Now that he'd had a sample of her sweetness and heat, he wanted all of it...all the time. Wanted to finally make her his in every way. Make up for hurting her, and all the lost years. But he'd never push her. He'd wait until she came around. And she would. She still had feelings for him. He saw them in her eyes, felt them in her touch. As long as they were around each other, spent time together, it was only a matter of time before she stopped fighting their attraction and opened up to him again.

This time, he wouldn't turn her down.

"You're sure Bella didn't see these?" Knight asked for the third time, motioning toward the monitor displaying the photographs he snapped of the IDs last night.

He nodded. "She was busy with the computers, and I kept my back to her while I took the photos." A slight smile tugged his lips. "Besides, do you really think she'd stay away if she knew?"

Bella was currently at her house, where he'd dropped her off last night. Hopefully, still sleeping. He'd caught a few hours of shut-eye after staying up most of the night, shifting through the evidence with Knight, hoping to figure out how and when Rasheed was arriving.

On his way to the apartment last night, after dropping Bella at home, he'd called Commander Lambert to fill him in about the IDs, and promised to send him a copy of the photos so Lambert could circulate them to all the agency heads.

This way, even if Matteo failed—which, hell fucking no, was not going to happen—there was no way Rasheed could go far without recognition software picking up his ugly mug.

He just wished the bastard would show up so he could get on with his mission already.

Matteo scrubbed a hand over his face before reaching for his fourth cup of coffee. It was almost time for his shift at the shop. Christ, he was tired. And today wasn't a good day to begin with. He just wanted to get through it without thinking too much. Experience had taught him the past few years that the key to getting through the anniversary of his mother's death was to keep busy.

This would be the first time he was actually home on the anniversary.

And in the actual house.

"Hell, no." Knight's chuckle snapped him out of his misery. "Bella wouldn't stay away. She'd be all over this evidence like white on rice, as the saying goes." His blue gaze sobered, and narrowed on the ID displayed on the monitor. "But, we need this bastard alive, not dead. I'm afraid Bella's philosophy is 'Ready. Shoot. Aim.' where Rasheed is concerned. It's a shame, though. We could use her help. She's a damn good tracker. One of the best I've ever worked with, if not *the* best."

He turned to face the commander and cocked his head. "About that. How exactly do you know Bella? Was she one of your agents?"

"Sort of." Knight smiled again, but this time admiration lit his gaze. "She's not a Knight, although, I'm working on that."

Which meant…

"You're saying you worked *with* her before you started your agency?"

"Yes."

Since the commander wasn't more forthcoming, Matteo immediately understood the meaning of his silence. "At Special Operations."

Knight smiled.

Damn. Bella was recruited into the S.O.G. Only the best of the best were sought.

Wait. He stiffened. "Is she still working for them?"

This time the commander shook his head. "No. She was recruited by a different department and left before I did."

"Left?" He frowned. "The CIA has her in a different department?"

Knight nodded. "Yeah, for several years now."

"Which department?"

"I'm afraid she was unable to disclose that when she left." His lips twitched.

Matteo raised a brow. "But you know anyhow, don't you?"

"Of course." Knight shrugged. "Like you, she was one of my team members. I make it a point to keep tabs on all of you."

A slight rippling of shock flickered through him. "You've kept tabs on every SEAL you've commanded?"

"Yes."

The man commanded several teams throughout his Navy career. "That's a lot, sir."

"Yes."

"Going to tell me who Bella works for?"

"No."

Damn. "Didn't think so." But it had been worth a try.

"Why does it matter?" Knight asked, closing the file on the computer, before heading to the coffee pot to refill his mug.

Matteo lifted a shoulder. "I just want to make sure someone has her back. She seems too used to working alone."

Knight sipped his coffee and nodded. "Her outfit conducts team and solo ops. From what I hear, she excels at the solo ones."

The memory of her sneaking into that damn building across the street flashed through his mind, and his body temperature shot up several degrees. "What outfit?"

A smile spread across the commander's lips. "Still as tenacious as ever, I see, Reaper."

"Yes, sir," he replied. "About that outfit?"

Chapter Ten

"It's so off the books and covert, it doesn't have a name," Knight told him.

Matteo's gut twisted tight. Son-of-a-bitch. He set his mug down on the counter hard. "Sounds like she's expendable."

"With both her parents gone, and no family to question her whereabouts...she's the perfect recruit. They all are, in that unit."

"Fuck." He ground his teeth and drew in a slow, steady breath.

It was his fault. He'd put her in this predicament. If only he hadn't shut her out. Left her behind. He should've faced his father and confessed his feelings for her. Christ, for all he knew, his dad might've been okay with it. Then Bella might not have joined the military at all. Never would've set out on the path that led to her doing a job where the outcome mattered more than the agent.

But would she have been cut out to be the wife of a SEAL? To sit at home while he took off without notice to places he couldn't disclose, and missions he couldn't discuss?

As much as Matteo knew she'd cared about him, he also knew that answer was no. She was too vivacious, too adventurous to sit idly by. It would've ended with her leaving him—tired and resentful—to go off and see the world. Alone.

"Yeah." Knight nodded, lifted his mug in a mock toast. "Now you see why I'm trying to recruit her."

Matteo blinked and refocused on the commander. "How can I help?"

"By doing what you've been doing this week," Knight replied. "What we've all been doing. Reminding her that working with a team is better. That someone having her back makes her stronger. That there's strength in a team."

He shoved a hand through his hair and gripped the back of his neck. "Keeping her out of the loop about Rasheed isn't going to win us any points."

Or help him break through the walls around her heart.

"When she finds out—because she *will* find out…she's even more tenacious than you—we'll just have to make her see why the bastard's more important alive," Knight said. "She'll come around. Trust me."

God, he wished he was as confident as the commander. All Matteo knew was he'd hurt her before, and didn't want to do it anymore.

The key sounded in the lock in the apartment door a second before it opened and Brooke and Bella walked in.

"Look who I found pulling up outside." Brooke smiled, but alarm drifted through her gaze as she glanced at the computers.

Thank Christ the commander had closed that damn file.

"Morning, Bella." Knight smiled. "There's fresh coffee. Help yourself."

"Thanks." She nodded, then glanced at him as she neared, concern darkening her gaze. "You okay? You look tired."

He nodded, stifling a yawn. "Yeah. Just tired. Stayed up late going over evidence."

Her eyebrows lowered and pinched together. "Why didn't you ask me? I would've helped."

Dammit. He had shit for brains.

"I called him here," the commander spoke up. "The Knight Agency is helping him with his mission. If you were one of my agents, I would've gladly called you in, too."

A smile spread across her lips. "I see what you did there. You are persistent."

"When have you known me not to be?" Knight smirked.

"Never." Her smile remained. "And I'm pretty certain I wasn't one of your agents last night either, and yet, you didn't seem to have an issue with me helping out."

"Ah, but that's different." The commander's smirk increased. "I needed you to get my agent inside."

She threw her head back and laughed. "Ah. I see how it is."

"I was also hoping you'd get a taste of how good it could be working with a partner or two," Knight stated, and Matteo nearly choked on the mouthful of coffee he tried to swallow.

The feel of her soft curves pressed against him, and taste of her hot, eager mouth immediately came to mind. Bella's gaze flicked to Matteo, and he knew she was remembering their kisses too.

"From what I hear, you both handled each other well," Knight added.

Matteo wondered if the man had seen the footage or heard the tapes, or if Brooke had filled the commander in on their heated *improvising*, but Knight's gaze remained neutral and gave nothing away.

"Yes." Bella nodded, her gaze finding his again. "Matteo proved to be very capable in a heated situation."

Oh, the woman had no idea.

He grinned and stepped closer. "Thank you. I was thinking the same about you."

Her lips parted into a sweet, sexy grin. "Good to know."

It was the warmth and motivation Matteo needed to head out and make pizza. But even when he was there slinging dough, he always kept his ears open and continued to work the mission.

An unease hoovered on the boardwalk lately. A tangible gnawing he felt growing stronger each day. The fact Paresh and his two pals stopped in the same time every day—a classic sign they were casing a job—sent up several red flags. If they hadn't already been under surveillance, he would've added them to the list.

And even though Paresh wasn't sleeping at the abandoned building, or carrying a backpack, it didn't stop them from watching him. Brooke oversaw keeping an eye on the kid, which eased some of Matteo's guilt about surveilling his friend's son whenever he talked with Omar.

"So, how is the mission going?" Bella asked as she poured a cup of coffee. "Did you find anything on the computers yet? Or in the photographs Matteo shot?"

His cue to leave. The less he had to lie to her the better. "I have to go open the shop," he said, slipping into his coat. "Let me know if anything comes up, otherwise, I'll see you tonight."

"Don't come back without a pepperoni and onion pizza," Knight told him.

"And green peppers," Brooke added.

He grinned. "Roger that." Then turned his attention to Bella. "Anything special you'd like to add?"

For a split second, heat flickered through her gaze, then disappeared. "You know what I like."

He was starting to, and looked forward to discovering all her secret turn-ons—what made her moan, what made her pant, and what made her cry out his name.

***

After spending the morning watching live feed of Tariq and Kamal reading in their room in the abandoned building—where the only action taking place was the paint literally peeling off the damn walls—Bella grabbed her coat from the back of the chair and slipped it on.

"Have fun," she told Knight and Brooke as she slung her backpack over her shoulder.

Knight transferred his attention from the monitor to her and lifted a brow. "Too much excitement?"

She snickered. "Yeah. I'll leave that fascinating bit of investigation to you."

"Going to sniff out a lead?" A knowing gleam entered Brooke's eyes.

Bella crossed her fingers behind her back, because everyone knew that made an outright lie more of a little fib. "Nah. I'm not technically a Knight, so I'm going to go home and do some laundry."

Brooke's snort echoed through the room. "Right."

It was good to hear her friend laugh. She didn't do it often enough.

And by laundry, she meant she was going to head to Camden to check out the gun shop where the two stars of the Taliq and Kamal show got their guns.

Knight frowned. "Why don't you wait for Matteo?"

Wait?

She raised her brows. "Because I'm wearing my big-girl panties today, and can handle a little laundry on my own. But don't worry, I'll be back before he finishes work and shows up with the pizza."

Disappointment flickered through Knight's eyes, and without permission, regret whispered through her body. Stupid emotion. Bella straightened her shoulders and walked out the door. He wasn't her boss anymore. She didn't need to please or impress him.

Then why was there a knot of remorse lodged in her chest?

On her drive into Camden, Bella contemplated the question and came up with a simple answer. Because she respected him and not having his approval didn't sit well in her gut.

But she had a mission to do, handed to her by her current boss. A mission she wanted—no, needed—to carry out on her own.

Helping Matteo and Knight was fun, but that wasn't her sole reason. She wasn't stupid. Even though they never said his name, she knew they were after Rasheed. So by sticking close to them, helping them out, she was hoping they would eventually lead her to her mark.

And it appeared to be paying off. Those IDs Matteo found in Simpson's filing cabinet last night—the one's he'd neglected to share with her—proved Rasheed was indeed coming to her hometown.

Having worked with Knight, Bella knew about the app his agents used, and in case Matteo was in possession of it, she'd used one of her CIA issued gadgets to target his phone when they'd danced last night. Being in his arms, pressed against his hard body had been amazing, and dangerously distracting. Good thing her gadget was automated and only needed to be within a few inches to reprogram the app on his phone to send a copy of anything that passed through his camera straight to her laptop at home.

A measure of guilt over deceiving him had gripped her chest during the party, but it'd dissipated the instant she'd arrived home last night to find a folder with photos of IDs with a bald, clean-shaven Rasheed in her inbox.

She didn't get mad, though. It was Matteo's job. His mission. She understood this and didn't take it personally. Using the device on him wasn't personal either. Just part of her job.

Like investigating the gun shop where she'd just arrived. The one Knight's people had determined was the place the weapons came from that Kamal and Taliq had hidden in their floor boards.

Contrary to Knight's suggestion, she didn't need hand-holding in order to investigate. Even if holding Matteo's hand had sent a delicious, tingling awareness throughout her body, making her wonder exactly how those big, firm, calloused hands would feel on her actual body.

Exhaling on a growl, she pushed those distracting thoughts aside, and returned her focus to her job at hand. Checking out the gun shop.

She knew when to observe, and when to engage, and when to shake the tree to see what nuts shook loose—today's goal.

Walking between a gorgeous sports car and a beat-up pickup, she found it amusing that a guy in a suit sat behind the wheel of the truck instead of the Jag.

Perhaps clothes were more important than the ride. Or perhaps the hair on the back of her neck was standing up for a reason.

Entering the shop, she noted five people, security cameras in every corner, a closed door to a room in back, and two burned-out bulbs in the ceiling, all before she shut the door.

A middle-aged man with a broken left thumb worked behind the counter, a young couple browsed handgun choices in the glass case that ran the whole left side of the shop, a guy in an expensive suit, like the one in the truck, talked on the phone, and a large man in a green sweater with a hole near the bottom stocked a shelf with boxes of pipe cleaners.

Nothing out of the ordinary.

She headed straight to guy behind the counter. "Hi. Maybe you can help me."

"I can try." His gaze twinkled when he smiled. "What can I do for you?"

"Have you seen either of these two men?" She pulled out her phone and showed him the screen. "They go by either Tariq and Kamal, or Kevin and Ron."

Everyone in the shop stopped what they were doing to glance her way. Exactly what she'd wanted, and reason for her loud, clear, tone.

He nodded. "Yeah. Kevin and Ron were in here last week. Why?" Dread erased his pleasant expression and wrinkled his brow. "Did they do something bad with the guns?"

"No." She slipped her phone back in her pocket. "Not yet. Just trying to find them before they do." A blatant lie to throw off anyone who could be listening. "Any chance you have an address for either of them?"

Not that she needed it. Knight's people already had a copy of the applications and had checked out the addresses. But she did need to shake that tree.

The guy narrowed his eyes and cocked his head. "You a cop or something?"

A smile tugged her lips. "Or something."

"I'm gonna need to see a badge before I give out that info."

"Of course." She handed him her credentials.

His brows rose, and posture straightened. "Yes, ma'am." He nodded, returning her ID. "I'll be right back with those addresses."

"Thank you." She smiled, and put away the badge she rarely used.

It wasn't exactly a shiny gold star with the words Terrorist Hunter on it, but the seal with U.S. Department of Homeland Security usually came in handy, even if her unit was technically a product of a joint operation between Homeland and the C.I.A.

"Here you go." The worker returned and handed her copies of the applications.

"I appreciate it." She folded the papers and shoved them in her jacket pocket, before pulling out a card and sliding it across the glass counter to him. "And if you see them again, I'd also appreciate if you'd call that number."

Not that she expected *Kevin* and *Ron* to show up again.

He glanced at the card before shoving it in his shirt pocket. "Of course."

She smiled at him. "Thank you. You've been very cooperative."

He nodded, and she took one last glance around the shop, hiding a smile as four onlookers immediately averted their gazes.

Perhaps she'd shaken something loose.

On her deliberately slow drive back to AC, Bella checked her rearview several times, satisfaction heating her blood as the familiar beat-up pickup from the gun shop parking lot followed at a distance, with a passenger now in the truck too.

When it didn't appear as if traffic was going to thin out, she turned off the expressway to lure the men away from the possibility of the innocent getting hurt.

The truck followed.

Good. Slowing to pay the toll at the end of the exit ramp, she glanced in her rearview and recognized the passenger as the man in the suit who'd been on the phone in the shop. Yeah, they didn't stand out or anything. Not with their suits appearing to cost more than the truck.

Idiots.

She turned right, then made a left onto a quiet service road that ran parallel to the expressway, separated by a thicket of woods.

Again, the truck followed.

The hair on the back of her neck stood up again. There was only one oncoming car, after that, the road would be deserted.

Perfect.

Without changing her posture so as not to give away her actions, she pressed the button to lower the window, then carefully reached for the gun holstered under her coat and flicked off the safety.

Adrenaline rushed through her veins, pounding through her chest with a familiar rhythm.

Things were about to get real.

Chapter Eleven

Once the road was clear in both directions, the truck swerved into the other lane and sped up to pull alongside her car. The man from the gun shop leveled a weapon at her through his open window.

"Hi, sweetheart." He grinned.

Bella squeezed the trigger on her Sig, already aimed at his head. "Bye, dickhead."

He slumped to the side, giving her a clear shot at the driver. Without missing a beat, she squeezed off two more rounds before slowing down. The truck veered to the left, hit a small ditch, and eventually rolled to a stop by a clump of trees.

She pulled to the side, grabbed her backpack, and raced to check the men for pulses. Finding none, she holstered her weapon, fished a scanner from her bag, then pressed each of their thumbs onto the screen, and frowned at their identities.

Russians?

Cursing under her breath, she rifled through the nearest mobster's pocket, pulled out his phone, and dialed her boss.

"Need a cleanup crew for the two dead Russians cluttering the Service Road in Hammonton. I just sent you their thumbprints."

"Did you say Russians?"

"Yep. Shook them loose at a gun shop in Camden." She pulled out her own phone and took several photos of the men while she talked. "There's plenty of open field for an in and out sweep. The crew can track this number for exact location."

"Roger. Anything new on Rasheed?"

She'd forwarded the ID photos to him last night. A flood of frustration tightened her chest. "Negative."

Unless Knight discovered something while she was away.

"We'll analyze this new development and get back to you," her boss stated. "Out."

"Roger. Out." She hung up, and tossed the dead Russian's phone onto his chest, then glanced at her own phone in her other hand.

Shit. She picked up her pace. She was going to be late.

Normally Bella wouldn't care, but today was the anniversary of Mrs. Santarelli's death, and she wanted to make sure he wasn't left alone, or tried to skip out on them.

Pushing the speed limit, Bella managed to get back to the apartment in record time, but not quickly enough. Matteo was getting out of his car as she pulled in behind him.

The setting sun cast an orange glow that competed with the brilliance of his grin. Shit. She sat up with a start. He was turning her mind sappy again. Freakin' sexy frogman.

With a shake of her head, she got out of the car and met him on the sidewalk where he stood waiting for her.

"Hey, beautiful." His tone was as warm as his gaze, and dammit, just like that, her heart skipped a beat, and whole body softened.

Clearing her suddenly dry throat, Bella tried to think of something witty to say, but her damn mind snagged on the fact he looked good enough to eat. Probably the adrenaline getting in the way because she still hadn't quite come down off that high. Although, the way he stood with his coat open and the wind plastering his T-shirt against his powerful chest, showcasing the definition beneath didn't help.

But what really did her in was the tuft of dark hair that blew across his forehead, reminding her of a youthful Matteo and how he used to coax her into the ocean and they'd swim for hours and relax on the sand until the sun fell from the sky. Despite the tragedy in her life, he made her laugh. All the time. With him, she felt light and carefree and good.

God, she missed him. Missed her, too.

"Bella…" He sucked in a breath and stepped close. "What are you thinking?"

She shook her head, trying desperately to dispel the melancholy.

He lifted a hand and softly ran his knuckles down her cheek. "Look at me."

Without her permission, her damn gaze lifted to meet his, and all the youthful yearning and longing she'd suppressed for years suddenly reappeared. Reaching out, she set her hands on his chest, needing to touch something solid, needing him to ground her because she was feeling way too shaky for her liking.

"Tell me," he urged quietly.

The resurfacing of those feelings brought with it a flood of pain. "Did I even cross your mind once, Matteo?"

His gaze softened. "You never left it."

"Then why did you leave me?" Her voice came out hoarse, but she didn't care. She needed to know.

"Because I was a fool." He moved his hand to cup the side of her head and kissed the tip of her nose. "A damn fool."

"Good answer," she murmured right before his lips brushed hers. Awareness fluttered through her belly, reminding her how he used to make it feel like an invisible butterfly sanctuary in her youth.

But there was nothing youthful about his kiss. It was direct, persistent, like he knew what he wanted and went for it.

And damn, it was what she wanted too.

His fingers moved against her scalp and she melted. No warning. Her bones just melted clean away. Matteo changed the angle and proceeded to knock her off-kilter with a wet, hot, deep kiss that was good. So damn good. She gripped the lapel of his coat and pressed her tongue to his.

A sexy sound rumbled in his throat as he glided his other hand down to her hip and pulled her in closer. Then closer still. A rush seared through her still fluttering belly. She could feel his heart pounding at Mach speed, and every single delicious inch of him. And damn, the man had some amazing inches.

Bella was lost, spinning in the sensations that would surely drown her if she allowed. But before she could even contemplate her decision, a passing car honked its horn amid a chorus of catcalls and whistles.

***

Matteo drew back at the same time as Bella. They blinked at each other. That was when he remembered where they were, in the middle of the sidewalk, not far from terrorist sympathizers, out in the open, distracted—easy targets.

He muttered a curse. "Sorry." Leaning forward, he kissed her nose again. "I lose all sense of time and place when my lips are on you."

"Ditto." She nodded, drawing in a deep breath, apparently just as lost as he'd been. "We should probably grab the pizza from your car and get inside. I'm sure Knight is gnawing on his fists by now."

Laughing, he reached for her hand. "The pizza's already in there."

"It is?" She glanced at him and frowned. "Then why were you in your car?"

Walking with her to the building, he slid his arm around her and grinned. "I forgot my phone." He let go of her hand and opened the door, standing back for her to enter. She'd barely gotten inside the entrance when a white blur rushed toward their feet.

"Oh, dear...grab her! Don't let her outside!" An elderly woman stood in the doorway of an apartment across the hall, gripping several letters in one hand and a walker in the other, her eyes wide with horror.

Instinct kicking in, he reached down and came back up with a protesting fluffy white ball of fur.

"Oh...be careful," the older woman warbled.

A second later, he cradled the cat against his chest and spoke in a low and soothing tone, and just like that the screeching stopped, and a loud purr echoed through the hall.

"That's wonderful. Ms. Puss hardly ever purrs for strangers." The lady smiled.

Bella waived in a dismissive gesture. "He has that effect on females. He's Matteo and I'm Bella."

He wondered if that meant he had that effect on her.

"Nice to meet you. I'm Franny. And it's wonderful to see a kind, respectful couple move into this building."

The woman obviously missed their passionate display on the sidewalk a few minutes ago.

"Matteo, can you bring Ms. Puss in here for me?" Franny asked.

He nodded, stroking the cat. "Sure. No problem."

"Such a nice young man." The lady backed into her apartment. "Sorry. Had my dang hip replaced last month and I'm still getting used to this daggone thing."

"Take your time." He slowly followed her inside and stiffened.

The apartment was not what it had seemed on the outside.

Disgust soured his mouth. It was fucking wall-to-wall holiday wonderland. Every inch of Franny's apartment was decorated with lights and holly and ceramic Santa's. A tabletop tree twinkled in front of the window, surrounded by a miniature light-up village, and on the couch sat over a dozen knitted Christmas scarves.

Who needed that many scarves?

"Bella, can you shut the door, dear? That way Matteo can put Ms. Puss down."

Biting back a grin, she did as directed. "It's beautiful in here."

She would like it. Even with all her losses, she'd managed to somehow retain her Christmas spirit.

"Thank you." Franny beamed. "I'm eighty-four years old, with a no-good hip, but I'm not dead yet. I did it all myself. My children and grandchildren all moved out of state."

"I'm sorry."

He could tell by the sadness and longing clouding her gaze that she'd give anything to have her grandmother back. And her mom. And her dad.

Without question, he'd do anything to wind the clock back five years, just to see his mother one last time.

Franny shrugged. "It's okay. I Facetime with them and my grandkids."

Matteo was impressed. There were a lot of people her age who didn't know how to use a cell phone, let alone features like that on a smartphone.

"Besides." Franny smiled. "I have Ms. Puss to keep me company."

He nodded absently...still stroking the cat.

"You can put her down now." Bella came over to lightly touch his arm. Compassion filled her gaze.

"All right." He set the cat on the floor, and the feline rubbed around his leg twice before sauntering off into the other room.

"Thank you again, Matteo. I'd like to give you something for saving her." Franny shuffled over to the couch and grabbed a scarf off the cushion.

Oh, hell no.

"I save up every year to make these for my family and friends," she told them. "I'd like you to have one."

Damn. He held his hands up and shook his head. "That's not necessary, ma'am. I was glad to help."

"I insist. It would mean the world to me to actually see someone wearing one of my creations in person, instead of in a photograph, or on the screen of my phone." Then without waiting for him to refuse again, the woman shuffled right up to him and looped it around his damn neck.

Bella bit her lips but he still heard her snicker. He glanced down at the black scarf with red reindeer and tried desperately to think of a way to take it off and leave it without offending the poor lady.

"Look how great that goes with your coat, Matteo," Bella said, with a grin. Damn woman was enjoying his discomfort way too much. "Such a generous gift. Thank you, Franny. I'm sure he'll treasure it."

The trick was going to be keeping him from tossing it away once they got upstairs.

"And I'll treasure seeing him wear it every day." Franny clapped her hands, her blue gaze warm and over bright with tears. "You remind me of my grandson, Patrick."

Ah, hell. She had to bring tears into it, and play the grandson card. Now he had to wear it. He couldn't deliberately break the old woman's heart.

Matteo cleared his throat. "Thank you, ma'am." Sweat was starting to break out on his temple. "If you'll excuse us, we have to go."

He grabbed Bella's hand and practically dragged her into the hall, and didn't stop until they were upstairs, standing outside the apartment door. "Sorry." He released her hand and smiled. "I was on decoration overload. Besides, I'm starved."

She smiled back. "Me, too."

"Let's hope they left us some." He chuckled as he opened the door. There was a good chance they were too late.

"There you two are. I was wondering what happened…to…" Knight's words halted and he blinked before dividing his gaze between them.

Something in his face must've conveyed his reluctance to discuss the atrocity around his neck, because neither of them mentioned the scarf on the coat he quickly shed and tossed across the room onto the couch.

"Any pizza left?" Bella asked, shrugging her coat off and setting it on the back of one of the kitchen chairs.

Brooke nodded. "Yeah, we left you a half a pie."

He snorted. "Good thing I brought two." Or there'd be nothing left. Matteo chuckled pulling a chair out for Bella.

A shaft of warmth spread through her gaze. "Thank you."

"It's probably cold by now," Knight said.

"That's okay." He sat next to her and smiled. "Bella and I like cold pizza." They'd practically lived off it as kids.

While they ate, the other two remained by the computers and filled them in on the day's un-excitement. Not only were they watching feed on the building across the street, they now had access to Simpson's mansion.

"Nothing exciting happened at either place today," Knight informed in a dull tone. "The guys across the street mostly read or played handheld video games. And when they left, it was to meet Paresh for lunch at your shop, Matteo. Then they walked the boardwalk for an hour before Paresh went home, and the other two returned here."

Made no sense. They had to be missing something.

"And Simpson's place?" Matteo asked, reaching for the final slice of pizza the sweet woman just set on his plate.

"Nothing much. He was at work most of the day." Brooke nodded to another monitor with feed of a darkened office.

Bella grinned. "You've been busy." Envy ricocheted through her expression. "You snuck into his executive office at the casino."

Admiration washed through him. A huge challenge. One he got the impression she would've loved to have been in on.

"I had time to waste during lunch," Brooke replied. "Besides, you were off doing laundry."

Knight turned to stare right at Bella. "Must've been a big load. Is that why you were late?"

Bella shrugged. "I would've been here sooner, but traffic was murder."

Odd. He hadn't encountered too much on his way over, and he'd only arrived ten minutes before her.

"I wasn't all that late," she said. "Matteo and I were downstairs helping one of the tenants with her cat. She was sweet. And grateful. She gave poor Matteo that scarf to wear, and expects to see it on him all the time."

He shifted in his chair. "Don't remind me."

"Well, I think it's cute." She grinned, getting up to clear the table.

Cute was not the word he would choose. He rose to his feet and helped, before walking over to the monitors and gripping the back of an empty chair. Unease settled over his shoulders, while anger heated his blood. These men hurt his father, and now they were planning an attack in his city.

"Does Simpson have any ties with Russia?" Bella asked out of the blue.

He reeled back and turned to face her, along with Knight and Brooke.

She raised a brow. "What? It's a hunch."

Knight narrowed his gaze. "Hunch, my ass. But I'm guessing you can't talk about it, so thanks for the tip."

She nodded. "And thanks for the pizza." Her gaze met his as she reached for her coat. "I have to go, but if you need company later, just knock."

Understanding softened her gaze, and he knew that wasn't a sexual proposition. It had nothing to do with sex and everything to do with friendship, and the fact it was a hard day because of the loss of his mother.

Touched by her unexpected show of concern and that she'd expressed it in front of an audience, he stepped close to help her into her coat, and to touch her, needing the physical connection to solidify the emotional one flowing between them.

His feelings for her increased — if that were possible — and Matteo knew his days of fighting their connection were over.

He loved her. And soon he was going to tell her. And show her. And beg her forgiveness for the past…and for Rasheed.

But for now, he'd have to settle for squeezing her shoulder. "Thank you," he said, turning her to face him. "I appreciate it."

A warm smile eased across her face. "I'll see you later."

Count on it. He nodded and forced his hands to release her. But only physically because she still had a grip on his thoughts long after she'd left. And after an hour and half of phone calls and back-tracking paper trails that yielded nothing extra, he rose to his feet and stretched the kinks out of his back.

"Go home, Reaper," Knight said, getting up to put on another pot of coffee. "There's nothing pressing going on. Brooke and I can handle the surveillance. Go get some rest. You look beat."

He suddenly felt drained. "Will do," he replied, shoving his coat on, too tired to even give a shit about the festive scarf around his neck.

All he knew was he had to see Bella, and the urge had nothing to do with any fear for her well-being. In fact, it had to do with his. But first, he needed to make a stop. One he'd been putting off all day.

An hour later, he sat in the car and stared at his house. It was dark, unlike most of the others on his street. Festive lights adorned porches and trees and yards in a show of holiday cheer. Even Bella had a wreath on her door and lights wrapped around her porch railing, and she'd suffered a hell of a lot more losses over the years than he had, and yet, she still celebrated.

His yard reflected his cheer. He had none. What little he'd ever had had died with his mom. She was the one with all the cheer. Hell, his dad had always joked she'd had enough for the whole family.

God, he missed that. He missed her. Guilt clawed at his gut and weighed heavily in his chest for not coming home more often. His fault. An airplane could've gotten him back to base in time if he'd been called up. And the worst part was he could fly, he just never bothered to go through testing to get his license. There were a lot of things he'd never bothered to do that he'd wanted. It was time to change that because regrets sucked. And he refused to have any more — starting with Bella.

He glanced at her house.

If you need company later, just knock.

Her invitation drifted through his mind. Lord knew he wanted to take her up on it, but it was late. Later than he'd expected to get home. He'd sat by his mother's grave a lot longer than planned.

With a sigh, he got out of his car and ordered his feet to head home, but somehow, he ended up in front of Bella's door. Christ, he didn't even remember knocking, but he must have, because it opened, and without a word, she smiled and stood aside to let him in.

Chapter Twelve

God…Matteo was so damn good-looking it almost hurt to look at him. Those dark eyes that normally held his emotions and secrets in check had been nothing but open and full of heat and longing and need since he'd returned.

All week long, she'd fought an inner battle to give in to her long-suppressed feelings for him again, while the survivor in her said hell no, not again.

But it was getting tougher to resist every day. Especially when he looked at her like she was his everything—the look she'd fantasized about seeing for years—the one he gave her right now.

Damn. A tremor shivered down her spine. He made it so hard to look away.

So she didn't.

"You okay?" She helped him out of his coat without asking, and set it on the back of a chair.

The way he'd sat in his car, staring at his house for the past fifteen minutes, cracked her heart wide open. She tried to force herself to stop watching him, but nothing made her move. Not until he'd gotten out and walked to her. Sought her out. He came to her. Not the other way around, as it had been in the past.

He wanted her. Needed her.

Her stomach fluttered at the thought. But she wasn't sure that was a good idea, nor was she thinking straight, so she didn't exactly trust her thoughts.

She was just going to have to go with her instincts.

He reached for her, gripping her hips as he slowly drew her closer. "I'm better now." Setting his forehead to hers, he closed his eyes and let out a long, deep breath, and she felt his whole body relax against her. "Much better."

Her hands automatically went to his chest. He was wonderfully warm and hard beneath her palms. This was probably not a good idea, but he opened his eyes and her misgivings disappeared under the warm, delicious intent in his gaze as he slowly lowered his head.

He brushed one corner of her mouth with his lips, and then the other, and nibbled and tasted in between. A soft sound rolled in her throat, and she clutched at his shirt, her whole body shaking in anticipation. Then he sealed his mouth to hers and slowly, thoroughly, kissed the strength from her limbs.

The other kisses she'd shared with him had been amazing, but this one...this was different. More. Fuller. Stronger. It was everything she'd always imagined, and more. Everything she wanted. And better.

Everything he should've given her long ago.

All the insecurity and pain from the past crashed through her. She broke the kiss and stepped back, needing to find her equilibrium, which was in no way, shape, or form near that man.

"Bella?" He reached for her, but she backed away.

"I...that felt..." She sucked in a breath and shook her head. "I can't go there again, Matteo. You left me. God, that hurt. What you were just giving and asking...I can't open myself up to that again."

"What is it you're afraid of?"

Her chest was squeezed so tight with remembered pain her voice was barely above a whisper. "That I'll let you in, give you everything...then you'll leave me again."

There would be no surviving it a second time. Hell, she'd barely managed it the first time around and they'd never even kissed.

Stepping close, he thrust his hands into her hair and cupped her head. "I'm done running, Bella. I swear it. I'm done running...unless it's to you." Intense and fierce, his gaze matched the conviction in his tone, and heaven help her, she felt both to the deepest depths of her darkened soul.

"I want to believe you." Okay, she did believe him, but dammit, she was scared.

His thumb lightly skipped over her cheek. "I was a fool to leave you before, and God, I'm so sorry I hurt you. But I promise, I will never do it again, baby. I'll never willingly leave you again."

Then he was kissing her with equal conviction, sweet and sincere, then hot and intense, embodying everything she felt for him, and from him all these years. And Bella was lost. Totally and irrevocably lost. And she didn't care. She deserved this. Wanted this. Dammit, she'd waited a lifetime for this man. She couldn't deny herself the pleasure of Matteo, not now that he wasn't holding back either.

Without breaking the kiss, he backed her up until she felt the living room wall behind her, and then he pressed into her and changed the angle of the kiss. It was a hot, intense tangle of tongues and hunger and needy sounds that echoed around and through them. He kissed her again. And again. And again. And he didn't stop until she was completely and utterly one hundred percent upside down and inside out.

When he finally broke the kiss, she took a second, or maybe a minute, before she opened her eyes. His gaze was deliciously dark and heated, and a sexy, dangerous grin tugged his lips. "We're doing that again."

"Damn straight," she uttered, with a matching grin, reaching up to shove her hands in his hair and hold him still while she brought her mouth to his and kissed him until they were both starved for air.

Sucking in a breath, he set his head against hers and muttered an oath, "We're probably going to kill each other."

She laughed, in total agreement. "I know. But what a way to go."

Then they lunged for each other again, and they were kissing, and removing shirts in a flurry of movement. He drew back to stare at her standing in her black bra, no shoes, and jeans with the top button undone. By him.

She smiled and ran her finger down his ridges and muscles, loving how his abs quivered under her touch. "You need to lose these," she said, unzipping his jeans and tugging them down, taking everything underneath with it, springing him free.

She knew he had great inches. She'd felt it, seen bulges, but the real, raw deal was magnificent.

"Bella."

She took him in her hands and he thunked his head back against the wall and closed his eyes, but when she covered the tip with her mouth, his eyes snapped open, and a raw, primal, need consumed his gaze.

He grabbed her shoulders and drew her to her feet. "My turn."

In a matter of seconds he had her stripped of her jeans, and his fingers underneath the straps of her bra, tugging them down her arms, until she bounced free. His chest rose and gaze heated as he watched her breasts bounce in place. "Beautiful," he murmured, before dipping down to cover one of her nipples with his mouth, while

he brushed his thumb over the other. She moaned and cupped both his head and his hand as they worked to drive her completely mad.

"Matteo," she gasped, when he changed sides and sucked the other nipple into his mouth.

Then his hands slid down her body, stroking and teasing, slipping his fingers under the edge of her panties, ripping a breathless, needy sound from her throat as he brushed the parts that ached for him the most. But then he moved his hand to grasp the black lace and tug it off her body.

He sucked in a breath and stared up at her. "God, Bella, you're beautiful." His gaze was full of heat and adoration, and she shook from the intensity of his emotions.

Starting at her calves, he ran his hands up her legs, over the curve of her hips, and brushed the sides of her breasts as he stood. Then his hand moved to her neck, while he pressed a path of hot open-mouthed kisses up the other side of her throat to her lips. The feel of his bare chest brushing hers sent a wave of heated sensation all the way down to her toes.

Looking into her eyes, he drew back and stroked his thumb lightly over her lower lip. "I want to hold you and taste you and make you want only me."

She glided her hands up his sides. "Matteo, I've only ever wanted you."

A look of fierce, primal emotion flared in his eyes a second before he captured her mouth for a deliciously thorough, deep, branding-type kiss. Moaning, she rocked into him, but he released her and drew back to sweep her off her feet and carry her into the hallway.

"Which door?" he asked, in a voice as strained as her breathing.

"End of the hall." When she'd moved back in two years ago, she'd taken over her grandmother's old room because it had a bathroom attached. She had every intention of making good use of that bathroom with Matteo tonight.

He set her on the bed, and explored her body, making her gasp as heat and need collided inside her. Bella could barely breathe, couldn't get enough air into her lungs, he had her quivering with need, shivering with goose bumps while heat scorched her veins.

Damn, adrenaline had nothing on Matteo.

She must've made some kind of sound because he stopped and glanced up from where he'd been grazing his spectacular, silky, soft bearded jaw against her inner thigh.

"You doing okay?"

She reached down to slide her hands into his hair. "Yes, keep going."

He chuckled and lowered his face back to her leg, where he kissed and licked and nipped until he had her squirming and gasping and swearing when he stopped just below her very best parts. She opened her eyes and met his gaze.

Her heart rocked and slipped into place at the emotion there, fierce, raw, unspoken but as real as the beat of her heart. She opened her mouth to say—who the hell knew what—but then he lowered his head again, and brushed her center with his lips.

"Matteo—" She tightened her grip on his hair, needing him to…needing more.

"I know." His breath was warm and erotic on her sensitized flesh. "I know, baby, but I've dreamt of this for so long. I'm not rushing this. I want to savor—"

His hands slid over her body, while his mouth teased, just on the edge. Just out of reach.

"Matteo," she ground out, aching and needing more.

Another chuckle vibrated through him, but he brought his hands down to help drive her mad, so she decided not to maim him. He spread her legs and sucked in a breath. "Gorgeous."

He looked his fill, and just when she thought she was going to have to encourage him to take action, he stroked her with a finger. Bella gasped and arched her head back, closing her eyes to enjoy the feel of his touch. He traced her folds up and down, making her squirm, until he finally slipped inside.

"Matteo," she cried out and shamelessly ground her hips, encouraging more.

He gave it to her, stroking her harder, faster, then gripped her hips with his hands and used his tongue to take her the rest of the way home. Which he did, with a thorough and exquisite precision that had her crying out his name in a long, drawn out moan as she shuddered with a release much stronger than any she'd ever experienced before.

After he let her down slowly, and she returned to planet earth, Bella opened her eyes and found Matteo regarding her with a smug smile on his talented lips and satisfaction smoldering in his eyes. "You taste sweeter than I ever imagined. And I can't wait to be inside you."

The force of emotion in his words and tone grounded Bella, filling her with an unexpected sense of contentment she hadn't realized was missing from her life. Until now.

Until Matteo.

***

"I want that too. But first, I get to taste, too." She smiled, then flipped him onto his back, and Matteo allowed it for a moment.

He let her hold him down and kiss him, because, hell—he couldn't get enough of that, or her, or the feel of her hair brushing his face. He loved the coconut scent of it—reminded him of summers and sunshine and ocean. He loved the feel of her soft curves pressing against him, the way her nipples scraped his chest with each delectable movement. The way her tongue brushed his, demanding and taking in a maneuver he was more than happy to give his full cooperation.

With a soft tug on his lower lip, she released his mouth to kiss her way down his body, nipping and licking, creating a fiery path straight down to his groin. Anticipation tripped his heart as her fingers and mouth hovered just shy of his throbbing erection.

Then she licked his length and he hissed out a breath when she suddenly took him into her mouth.

Fuck. "That feels good," he muttered, closing his eyes as he set his hands on her head and ran his fingers through her hair.

"Mmm..." she moaned, and ah, hell, he nearly lost his mind.

Tightening his hold on her, he opened his eyes and looked down to watch her work him over. Her hair spilled over his groin, and hands gripped his hips while her breasts brushed his legs in her enthusiasm.

As if sensing his appraisal, she flicked her gaze to him without stopping her ministrations, and a wicked gleam entered her eyes, turning them a decadent emerald. His insides fisted tight.

With a groan, he pulled her up his body, then rolled, tucking her beneath him before he lost control.

"Hey." She chuckled. "I wasn't finished."

The disappointment in her tone was mirrored in her emerald eyes and it nearly did him in. His body was hard and mouth was dry.

"I almost was." He kissed her neck, then made his way to her shoulder, her collarbone, then moved lower to flick his tongue over her stiff nipple, before sucking it into his mouth.

She drew in a breath and her hands cupped his head as if afraid he was going to leave.

No way. "I'm not going anywhere," he told her.

He was never leaving her again. Ever. He rasped his tongue over her other nipple. This time she moaned and arched up into him. She was so damn responsive. He rocked his hips, pressing her back down into the bed.

"Matteo." She writhed beneath him, making soft, sensuous sounds that tested his tenuous control. He lifted his head to stare down at her. Head back, eyes closed, bottom lip pulled between her teeth…damn, she was so beautiful, and every man's secret fantasy.

She sure as hell had always been his, but what was even better than that was the fact she was his amazing reality.

He dipped down and sucked that bottom lip of hers into his mouth, then soothed it with his tongue. She lifted her hips and moaned.

Hard and throbbing, he went to roll off to fetch a condom…when he remembered he didn't have any. Not something he carried around often.

"What's wrong?" She frowned, running her hand over his shoulder.

"I just remembered I don't have a condom." He took in the disappointment clouding her gaze, and he blew out a breath. "Don't suppose you have one?"

She shook her head. "Nope." Then pulled him back down on her. "I'm clean. On birth control. And need you in me now, Matteo. I've waited way too long to let a condom get in the way." She blinked a second before she snickered.

He laughed too, then choked on it as she stroked him back to throbbing. "Bella—"

"Mmm..." She spread her legs and glanced up at him. "Don't you think it's time you made me yours, Matteo?"

"Yes." Hell, yeah. Settling between her legs, he positioned his tip near her center, and holding her gaze, he slowly pushed inside.

Fuck, she felt good.

"So good," she uttered on a hitched breath, echoing his thoughts while she clutched his shoulders and rocked her hips to take him in deeper.

"Bella..." Damn. He knew it would be this way. Knew she'd feel better than any other.

He grabbed her hands and held them on either side of her head, entwining their fingers together as he thrust into her, needing to feel everything, to give her everything.

The pull of their bodies increased the heat blazing inside him. He dipped down to capture her sighs in a kiss he craved more than air. Over and over, he tasted her heat and need, feeling her body quiver as she neared another release.

He broke the kiss and held her gaze, surprised to find hers open. As it always happened whenever she decided to drop her guard and let him in, he felt grounded, but this time, it was different. It was more, and that mere fact ratcheted up the desire coursing through him.

Matteo thrust into her, deep and fast. She was taking all of him now, and his gaze never left hers as he reached between them to brush a thumb over her center, and sent her over the edge.

She cried out his name, and the sound of it and feel of her pulsing around him was so exquisite he wished he could savor it forever, but it was too much. Too good. Too damn perfect. He pushed inside her one last time and let go with her, both their worlds crashing apart, then coming back together.

Stronger.

Better.

Whole.

When he mustered enough energy to move, Matteo rolled to his side and pulled Bella with him, so she sprawled half over him. He slowly guided his hand up and down her still-trembling body. "You with me?"

"Always." She snuggled close, pressing her face into his throat, her breath warming him in spurts. "You were amazing."

Satisfaction filled him to near bursting. He tightened his hold on her. "So were you, but I always knew it would be incredible between us."

"Are you sure it wasn't just because it was unprotected?"

"Positive. The rush was unparalleled way before I entered you."

"For me, too. I tried to get you to listen." She playfully smacked his chest.

"I'm listening now," he said. "And I'm not ever letting you go, Bella."

She stilled a millisecond before burrowing closer. "Good to know."

Something in her tone still sounded a little unsure, and it about killed him. But he understood he was going to have to earn her trust.

"You know?" she said, drawing circles on his chest with her finger. "I've never had unprotected sex before."

"Neither have I." But, damn, it was something he definitely wanted to do again with her.

He could feel her grin against his skin. "See that? We are each other's first after all."

He tipped them so that he could look into her eyes as she rested in the crook of his arm. "And we're going to be each other's lasts."

The most beautiful smile spread across her face and his heart rocked into his ribs. "Roger that."

***

Bella was afraid if she opened her eyes she'd find that last night was just another delicious dream, like all the others she'd had about Matteo over the years. And in truth, she didn't think she could bear the disappointment right now. God, not after what they'd shared last night.

Just in case it hadn't been real, she decided to give herself another five minutes of snuggling into the furnace of hot male who was asleep partially beneath and around her, since she had twisted herself around him like a pretzel.

Even in her subconscious, it was almost as if she didn't want to let him go, either.

"Going to open your eyes anytime soon, baby?" Matteo's sexy, low, morning voice caused her whole body to tremble, and the brush of his mouth near her ear wasn't bad either.

She opened her eyes to see he, indeed, was real. And she should've known, because last night had been way better than any fantasy she'd ever imagined with Matteo.

"Morning." Leaning forward, she kissed his sexy, scruff-covered jaw that had gotten an up-close-and-very-personal view of her entire body when he'd treated her to a head-to-toe body rub with his face. Twice.

The tactile memory of Matteo dragging his silky-soft, yet deliciously rough jaw across all her good parts caused a complete body quiver.

His hands tightened on her ass cheek and arm a second before he rolled them until he was on top of her with his mouth reacquainting itself with hers, because it'd been at least three hours since they'd gone at it.

"Good morning," he murmured when he broke the kiss.

"Mmm…" She smiled and trailed her hands down his chest to stroke his sides with her thumbs. "Love your good mornings as much as your good nights."

"Just wait until you experience my in-betweens," he teased, trailing kisses down her throat.

Sighing, she tightened her hold. "I already know you have great in-betweens, Matteo." Mega-incredible, mouthwatering in-betweens that had her sore—in a good way—and gave her the best up-against-the-shower wall-monkey-sex of her life. Twice. She was never going to look at her bathroom the same ever again.

In a good way.

While his mouth continued to blaze a trail southward, she could feel him smile against her belly. "Good to know." Nipping her hip, he shifted down and made himself at home between her thighs.

Breath caught in her throat as heat spread through her body in a fluttering rush.

"I much prefer your *in-betweens*," he said. And then he proceeded to show her exactly how much.

In careful, diligent, in-depth detail.

Twice.

***

A few days later, Matteo was whistling to a tune he'd heard on the radio and slinging pizza, while keeping an eye on the boardwalk and the people walking by. Despite his good mood, he was filling with unease more and more every hour. It crackled down his spine, making him itch. Christmas was less than a week away, and he still had no damn idea where Rasheed was, or his target.

So far, he sucked as a sleeper SEAL. Thankfully, Commander Lambert disagreed.

Even commended him the other day for his diligence.

But Matteo was a hell of a lot more capable, and not at all pleased with himself. Today was the last day he was tossing dough. He'd already lined up a replacement. Starting tomorrow, he was on Rasheed's trail, twenty-four/seven.

Well, with a little Bella downtime thrown in to keep him sane. Just the thought of their *downtime* every night since they stopped fighting their chemistry—and every morning—had him hard. Having decided not to rock the boat, they'd gone through a medium-sized box of condoms.

He smiled.

"Okay. What gives?" Omar asked as he watched him from the doorway.

Damn. How long had the man been standing there?'

"Hi, Omar. The usual?"

"But of course," his friend replied with a smile and a nod.

"How was your trip?" He'd been in New York a few days, helping his mother move in with her sister. "Is your mother settled in?"

"Yes. Thank you." Omar smiled. "My aunt will be thrilled to have a companion." The man studied him a moment. "You're very chipper. I don't think I've ever heard you whistle before, let alone a holiday tune."

Holiday tune?

He raised a brow. Could be. That was all the radio played these days. "A rarity for sure."

And Bella's fault. Her acceptance and forgiveness had put a perpetual grin in his heart. That, and the fact she rocked his damn world in and out of bed. A smile twitched his lips.

She'd been back in town a week, and managed to get him to reconcile himself with his past, and helped him to move forward. It was strange. He hadn't even known he'd needed to do that, and yet, it had happened. And with ease, too.

"He's been smiling like that all day. Heck, all week," Joe said, smirking near the drink station.

Omar lifted a brow. "Smiling and whistling?"

Working on the turkey wrap, Matteo rolled his eyes at the men gossiping like little girls.

"Yes." Joe nodded. "And he's wearing a scarf with reindeer on it."

It meant a lot to Franny, and Bella, so Matteo had seen no reason to remove it.

Omar reeled back. "No. I don't believe it."

"It's true. Look." Joe pulled out his phone and showed a picture the damn man had snapped of him the second he'd walked in that first morning after.

Matteo had still been operating in a post-climax state of mind to even notice. Bella had been extra adventurous right before he'd left for work.

He'd been ten minutes late opening the shop.

Worth every damn bit of the revenue loss.

"Only one thing could cause that much change to a confirmed Grinch," Omar said with a tilt of his head. "A woman."

Joe reeled back. "A woman? I haven't seen him with anyone, but I do agree with you."

"Only one woman could bring the life back to that face." Omar stabbed his thumb toward him. "Bella." He folded his arms across his chest and gave a firm nod of his head, as if daring him to tell him otherwise.

Matteo handed Omar his wrap and nodded. "You're right. There is only one Bella."

The man frowned. "Not sure that is what I said, but I am going to take that to mean I am right."

Omar and Joe continued to stare at him, as if waiting for confirmation. Matteo grabbed a ball of dough and slapped it on the counter. Blame it on his new outlook on life, or his night of incredible sex—either way, he was feeling generous.

He glanced at the men and grinned. "You're not wrong."

Omar slapped the counter. "I knew it. That's great news. And about time."

"He's only been back a few weeks." Joe frowned. "I've seen many guys work for months to try to coax her out on a date."

Heat spread down Matteo's shoulders and into his spine. He stiffened. "What guys? I want names."

Omar chuckled. "Down, boy." He turned to Joe and winked. "He's been in love with this girl since they were in school."

And since the man was dead-on, Matteo didn't even try to disagree. In fact, he took it a step further. "And an idiot for nearly a decade."

Joe walked over and slapped him on the back. "Never too late, man. That is great news. And Bella's a gem. You're a lucky man."

"I know." Damn lucky.

"Guess that means you won't be joining the Grinch Convention at the Capris this year." Joe chuckled, filling a cup with iced tea, before pushing it toward Omar.

"I think that would be a fun one to attend," Omar said, reaching for his drink. "My son got a job helping out at that convention."

Matteo froze, except for his pulse, which skyrocketed in an instant. Forcing his fingers to continue to work the dough, he glanced over at Omar. "Really? Which son?"

Chapter Thirteen

A certainty rushed through Matteo, and he knew the answer before his friend replied.

"Paresh." Omar smiled, unaware just how bad this was for his son.

But for Matteo's investigation, it was a blessing. The venue just became very clear, and halted their search. His gaze shifted to the convention flyer on the community board on the wall where his father happily allowed businesses to post upcoming events.

Then his insides stilled again. Is that what had happened that morning his father had been attacked? Had Paresh and his friends been hanging up the flyer and said something his father had overheard?

Made too much sense to Matteo for it not to be true.

Anger resurfaced, shaking through his hands. Hopefully his father would soon regain his speech ability. According to Knight, the doctors were close, and running tests on their concoction to work out possible side effects. It'd been a long month since his father's stroke/attack, but he was relieved to have him as far away from Atlantic City as possible at the moment.

Now, if only he could convince Bella to leave until after the New Year. A small smile tugged his lips. Like that would ever happen.

After Matteo shoved the pie in the oven, he headed to the office in back to make a few calls. First one was to Commander Lambert. Shutting the office door with his foot, he pulled out his phone, and dialed the man.

"Reaper," Lambert answered on the first ring. "Tell me you have something."

"I do, sir," he replied, and damn, it fucking rocked to have a solid lead. "The target is a convention being held at the Capris this coming Saturday."

"Scale of one to ten, how positive are you?"

"Ten, sir." No way was it a coincidence that Paresh just happened to land a job at one of the venues on their watch list. And with the help of his new friends.

"I understand you already have eyes on that place."

"Yes, sir." He nodded as if the man could see. Rolling his eyes at himself, he reached into the candy dish on the desk and grabbed a piece of taffy. "A…friend of mine works there. I'll see if I can get a tour of the rooms involved."

Matteo wasn't certain Bella had that kind of access, but this was Bella. Tugging the wrapper off the taffy he grinned. She didn't exactly always ask permission anyway.

The woman was impetuous and spontaneous, two traits that could be trouble, but she wore them well.

"Roger that," Lambert replied. "Since the event is only a few days away, Rasheed must be on his way, if not already there."

Twirling the candy in his fingers, he grimaced. The heat from his body warmed up the confection, making it sticky. But was that the reason for his sour expression? No. That was directed at himself and his inability to track down one damn man. "Agreed."

"Find him before Saturday."

"Yes, sir," he replied—to a dead call.

The commander had already hung up.

That went well.

Fuck. He popped the softened taffy in his mouth, needing the sweet treat to fight the sour taste the phone call left in his mouth. Spouting several silent curses—aimed at himself—he wiped his fingers on a leftover napkin from his lunch yesterday, tossed it, and his self-disparagement away, and got back to business.

He cleared his throat and dialed Knight.

"I heard. It's the Grinch Convention," the commander stated in greeting.

How the hell…?

Matteo shook his head and a small laugh rumbled in his throat. It was Jameson Knight. The man had connections even God didn't know about.

"Yeah." He nodded. "Omar just told me Paresh is working it. He could be our in if we need it."

"Agreed. We're switching our sole focus on the Capris as the venue now. And of course, we'll keep eyes on Simpson and the two sympathizers across the street here."

"Any word about those Russians?"

"Working on it."

Was it his imagination, or had there been a slight pause?

Again, he shook his head. Probably the former. "I'm heading over to the Capris now."

"Good," Knight said, a measure of relief in his tone that did the exact opposite to Matteo's nerves.

"Why? What's wrong? Is Bella okay?" She still had another half hour on her shift at the Capris.

"Nothing." Knight's chuckle rumbled through the phone. "Calm down, Romeo. She's fine. I was just referring to the fact we need to dig deeper now that we know the venue, and your going there now is good. You and Bella can snoop around."

Matteo let out a breath. "Roger that. Out."

***

The instant Bella walked into the Capris that morning, she knew today was going to be the day. An unease, like a thick, soaking wet, wool blanket, settled over her shoulders and chest. No sooner had Knight sent her a text about Paresh working the Grinch Convention, then he walked in.

Robert Johnson. A.K.A...Rasheed Al-Zahawi. Her mark.

Also fucking known as — her father's killer.

Bastard wore a smug grin as he walked right through the center of the casino and sat down at the next table. Bella wasn't sure if he knew who she was and he was being cocky, or if he was just that unlucky to pick her casino and the table next to hers.

Because he was definitely going to draw his last card today.

And his last breath.

With her backpack shoved in an employee locker, she was only armed with the Sig in her ankle holster, and the knife strapped to the other ankle. But, unlike Rasheed, she would never pick such a busy, public location to engage the asshole.

Her mind whirled with scenarios, and played them in her head, most coming to the same deadly outcome. Too many dead civilians.

Dammit.

She was not going to allow that man to leave her sight.

It wasn't his style to surround himself with a ton of bodyguards. Just a mystery partner. He usually eliminated the need for bodyguards by wrapping an explosive vest around his middle and covering it up under an expensive suit.

Like the one he was currently wearing.

Shit.

There was a holiday promotion going on, so the place was unusually packed for that time of the day. She glanced around the immediate area, and took in a quick head count. Damn. Easily in the triple digits, and that was just near the tables. The slot floor was much more crowded.

She delivered payouts, then dealt out another hand, grateful she didn't have any new players, or any cashing out. This gave her time to continue to observe him.

The suit was just bulky enough to set her hackles up. It was his M.O. to open it if confronted. She'd read the police report. That was exactly what had happened when her father and his partner had cornered the bastard in an alley two blocks from Times Square on that fateful New Year's Eve. They'd caught up with him after the police and Homeland had stopped the main plot that was supposed to involve massive explosives detonating when the ball dropped.

Rasheed had taken flight, but her father and his partner had chased him, unaware of the vest, until the bastard had opened his suit, threatening to press the switch on the detonator in his hand if they didn't lower their weapons.

They hadn't.

But Rasheed had a silent partner no one knew about—and a gun in his pocket—which he used to shoot her dad, who had been under fire from the mystery partner. The police shot and killed the partner, so Rasheed had held up his detonator, threatening to take everyone out, but the idiot had made the mistake of thinking her father dead. Not yet. He'd still had enough life in him to shoot Rasheed's hand clean off.

The police had subdued him after that, removed the vest and tossed his ass in jail. But the sneaky bastard had faithful followers, and eventually during the long trial, they made their move and busted him free—killing several law enforcement officers and nearby civilians in the process.

Bella dropped her gaze to the arm he had in a sling, no doubt for show. Alarm trickled down her spine at the thought of what he was hiding inside. She was pulling triple duty, watching the terrorist while dealing cards at her table, and surveying the area for signs of his latest silent partner.

It was against the rules to use her phone while dealing, so texting anyone was out of the question, but she didn't give a shit. And would've gladly texted Knight or Brooke or Matteo for backup, truly not caring who killed the bastard, but it was because of that very bastard she didn't pull out her phone. He had an equally good line of sight on her, and it would no doubt raise his suspicion to catch a Blackjack dealer using a phone. He'd clue in straight off that she was more than a dealer.

And the end of her shift didn't exactly help her predicament either. She'd be expected to leave the area, but there was no way she would. Apprehension gripped her chest with cruel fingers. No matter how she ran things in her head, nothing worked out with ease.

Throughout all this, she continued to deal. It was one of the more silent games, relying mostly on hand gestures than talking. This helped her as she tried to figure out how to get Rasheed away from the innocent and into her clutches so she could deliver his long awaited, sanctioned fate.

Four more minutes until her shift ended. Bella's heartbeat increased along with her concern. His stack of chips was dwindling. If he continued to lose at this rate, he'd be done before her shift ended.

Again, she tried to ascertain if he was that stupid, or just killing time to keep up appearances. As he lost his last few chips, she cursed her luck, because she still had a little over a minute left before she could leave without causing a commotion. Mentally crossing her fingers, she watched to see if he was going to put more money on the table.

He didn't.

Dammit.

He got up off his chair, and because she had no backup, Bella was faced with the possibility of losing him. Her stomach clenched tight. Not going to happen. She couldn't allow that— wouldn't allow that. No way was she permitting him to leave. She'd much prefer to tail him unobserved, but that didn't appear to be an option.

Until help arrived in the form of the very man who recently promised to always have her back.

Matteo.

The instant his gaze met hers, Bella knew the man got it. He knew something was up. His posture had switched from relaxed to SEAL in the blink of an eye. If she hadn't been on a mission—the most important one of her life— she would've found it hot as hell.

Okay, she did, but now wasn't the time. Rasheed was a few feet away, turning to leave.

But Bella didn't panic. Using her gaze, she pointed toward the bastard, and Matteo's gaze immediately followed. His chin lifted a fraction, and again, she knew he'd caught on. Spotted Rasheed.

He met her gaze briefly again, gave her a slight nod, then pulled out his phone and followed Rasheed through the casino. With less than a minute left of her shift, she finished dealing the hand to her table, acutely aware of her surroundings and everyone in them as she watched to see if anyone followed Matteo.

She didn't sense that Rasheed planned to target the casino today. Not with the convention a few days away. He wouldn't jeopardize that mission with another, especially in the same building a few days earlier, which would no doubt cancel the convention.

Unless he was cornered.

Her heart lurched. God, she hoped Matteo was careful. He'd read the police report and knew the circumstances of her father's death. He was a SEAL. He would be fine.

That was what Bella kept telling herself as she watched the man she loved disappear into the crowd while following the man she loathed.

The hand ended. Bella delivered the payouts and smiled when she received the tap she'd waited for on her shoulder.

Dealer change.

She made the universal sign of clearing her hands. "Thank you, gentlemen," she told the four men at her table with a smile. "Good luck." Then she stepped back and nodded to the new dealer, before switching into hunt mode.

Leaving the pit, she pulled the phone from her pocket and called Brooke. "Talk to me. Where is he?"

"Matteo's trunk."

Bella's steps faltered as shock rippled through her. "Already?"

Brooke's chuckle filled her ear. "He's a SEAL. Extensively trained."

Which meant quick, efficient. Deadly.

"Where's he taking him?"

Her heart thudded hard in her chest. She wanted in.

"I'll text you the address. Knight's at a meeting about the Russians. He'll catch up with you two when he's finished."

She stopped near the employee door. "Roger. Got eyes on me?"

"Affirmative."

"Did you notice anyone watching Rasheed or Matteo leave?" she asked, holding her breath.

"Negative. No one appeared to be interested. I'm going to go back and re-watch in a few."

She exhaled. "Roger. Out."

Her phone dinged with an incoming text. With Rasheed in Matteo's custody, she had the extra minute to grab her bag. Walking to the employee lockers, she glanced at Brooke's text and smiled.

Smart SEAL. The address where he'd taken Rasheed was in an unpopulated section abandoned after Hurricane Sandy's devastation, just a few miles up the road.

She nodded to a few coworkers as she grabbed her backpack. Adrenaline carried a heated rush she welcomed with smile.

Time for a face-to-*bullet* with Rasheed.

Chapter Fourteen

Matteo ended his update call with Lambert as he drove his car into the abandoned building through a large, gaping hole in the side of one wall. This place had immediately come to mind when Lambert had first told him about the mission. Matteo knew this site fit the bill for his purposes.

No eyes. No electricity. Concrete structure. What remained of this old shoe factory was sturdy, and the basement had three rooms and no windows or exits, other than the single stairwell that led down.

Perfect.

Since given the mission, he'd outfitted the place for his needs. All that was missing was Rasheed. Until now.

Matteo hoisted the bound, unconscious ass over his shoulder and carried him downstairs to his new home. An empty room, except for the hook he'd fashioned to hang from the steel beam in the middle of the ceiling.

Struggling with the dead weight, he muttered a few oaths before he finally managed to secure the man to the hook, via the zip tie binding his wrists. The task was easier with a partner.

Damn, he missed his team.

At least taking the guy down had been cake. Since the idiot traveled without a bodyguard, there'd been no obstacles. Once the man had stepped outside onto the boardwalk, Matteo had followed, injecting the man from behind with a knockout drug to eliminate a possible repeat of the New Year's Eve confrontation. It was the first thing he'd asked Knight to get.

Matteo had to admit it'd felt good to jab that needle in the man's vein. Sort of his own personal retribution for his father's injection. After that, he'd commissioned a rickshaw ride to the ramp closest to his vehicle, for him and his *inebriated friend*.

Standing back, he straightened his shirt, then stiffened at the sound of someone entering the room behind him. Then awareness skittered down his spine and he knew it was Bella.

"Step away from him, Matteo." Bella's tone was different. Hard. Cold.

Careful to keep his body between her and Rasheed, he twisted around to find a gun trained on him. "Bella. Put that away."

The wrinkling of her brow was the only movement. "Why? Did you kill him already?"

"No." He shook his head.

A smile pushed some of the chill from her gaze. But her aim remained. "You saved him for me?"

"No," he repeated, slowly stepping toward her. "Put the gun down."

Her smile disappeared. "Not until I shoot him."

"I can't let you do that."

Her head jerked back. "Why the hell not? It's sanctioned. He's my mark. I don't want to hurt you, Matteo. Now move."

"I can't. Just listen—" He didn't get to finish his sentence because she rolled to the side and fired off a shot as she came to her feet again.

The muffled sound of bullet hitting flesh echoed in the room.

Fuck.

"Bella. Stop!" He moved with her, keeping as much of his body as possible in front of the unconscious man. Matteo didn't have the time to check to see where the bullet hit, but he knew it hadn't been a kill shot because the trajectory from that angle only covered the lower torso and legs.

She rolled.

He moved.

She shot again, this time with no bullet impact. "Dammit, Matteo, move."

They did this dance two more times before he managed to get close enough to tackle her to the floor, knocking her gun away. "Hold on," he muttered, wrestling with her.

Damn, she was strong.

"He killed my father." She wriggled away.

Son-of-a-bitch.

He grasped her leg and pulled her underneath him, using his body to hold her down. "Bella. Stop." She thrashed, trying to work her legs free, but he knew that would mean a knee to groin. Although, he'd like to think she wouldn't pull that on him. "Stop." He grasped her wrists and held her hands above her head. "Listen."

"No, you listen." She stilled and stared into his eyes, hers still cold and determined. "I was commissioned to kill him. He's my job. My mission. And my revenge."

He blew out a breath. "I know. And you can have it. Just not today. We need to get information from him first. There are innocent lives at stake."

Her chin lifted slightly. That got her attention. "You know the venue?"

"Yes. The Grinch Convention," he replied. "But we don't know how or who he's working with. And you know as well as I do that killing him now is not going to stop that attack. We need that info."

"Shit." Her body slackened, and she blew out a breath.

"You can finish your mission. I promise," he said, easing his hold, just a little.

She blinked, and her gaze began to thaw. "Fine. But, I'll have to clear it with my boss first. Let me up."

He hesitated, studying her face, but he sensed she'd told him the truth. "Okay."

He released her wrists and rolled off to push to his feet, then offered his hand to help her up. For a brief moment, he wasn't sure she'd take it. His heartbeat slowed, but when she grasped his hand, it resumed beating at normal speed.

Once she retrieved her gun and holstered it, he waited until she was on the phone with her boss before he walked over to check on the Rasheed's still unconscious, but now-bleeding body.

A through-and-through in the thigh, missing the artery. Rasheed was damn lucky. So was Matteo. If that bullet had hit a quarter inch to the left, his mission would've died along with Rasheed, and countless innocent lives.

"Okay," Bella said, shoving her phone in her pocket as she neared. "The bastard's got a reprieve."

Her pupils were large and gaze unblinking as she stared at the man who'd murdered her father. Matteo couldn't even begin to know what she was thinking or feeling. He lifted a hand to lightly touch her back.

She was shaking.

His insides fisted tight. "I'm sorry," he said quietly. "I wouldn't have stopped you—"

"I know." She cut him off, but she hadn't shied away from his touch, so he'd take that as a win. "I wouldn't have shot around you if—"

"I know." That time, he cut her off. He knew this was a special circumstance, and he wasn't going to take the incident personally. He was curious about something else, though. "How did you know that was Rasheed? I mean, he looks quite different."

"I used a device that made your phone send me the photos you sent Knight at the party."

Well, hell.

"Sorry," she said, and they just stared at each other.

"SITREP," Knight said, striding into the room. One glance at Rasheed's bleeding, prone, hanging body sent the commander's eyebrows up. "Alive?"

"For now," Bella said.

Matteo motioned to the door with his nod of his head. "Let's take this in the other room."

"Roger that." Knight pivoted on his feet and marched from the room.

Matteo waited for Bella to do the same, before he picked up the rear.

"What's the plan?" she asked the second she entered the room across the hall with Knight.

"We have information about the Russians Bella killed," Knight stated.

He reeled back. "What?" He twisted to face her. "What does he mean you killed them?"

She shrugged. "It was either them or me. I chose me."

Jesus. His heart was squeezed so tight he could barely breath.

"They trafficked chemical weapons," Knight continued.

Now Matteo's heart fucking rocked. Chemical? This changed their search.

Bella stiffened. "What's missing?"

"Nerve gas."

Fuck.

He clenched his fists. "Any idea if those Russians had finished their business with Rasheed?" He was going to need time to process the Bella killing them "It was them or me" part.

"Yes." Knight nodded. "Every agency in the country, and outside of it, has been tracing their recent movements. It looks like the men had met with Kamal and Tariq last month."

"Could they have sold the gas to Simpson?" he asked, trying to figure out how the billionaire fit into all this mess. It made no sense why he'd willingly attack his own casino. But then again, if he was a terrorist, or a radical, their thinking was irrational at best.

"We're still trying to figure Simpson out." Knight ran a hand through his hair.

"So what now?" Bella asked, leaning against the wall, expression closed off.

Matteo wished he could hold her and make everything okay. Take away all the turmoil and pain he knew was swirling inside her.

The commander straightened his spine. "My people and I are going to work on getting Rasheed to talk."

She snorted. "Good luck. That bastard's not going to give you a damn thing."

He agreed. The likelihood of someone getting any information out of the heartless man was slim, even for someone as skilled as Knight.

"Still need to try," the commander said. "In the meantime, Bella, we need you and Matteo to search the Capris for that nerve gas. Homeland raided the abandoned building and took Tariq and Kamal into custody a half hour ago. Every agency has teams on the way. They'll start scouring the casino."

"What about Paresh?" he asked, as his gut tightened for Omar and his family.

"They have him, too. I'm sorry."

So was he, but it was out of his hands.

"And if Rasheed's secret partner notices the activity?"

Knight smiled. "He won't, because they'll all be dressed as the Grinch. Including you two."

Chapter Fifteen

Back at the apartment, Matteo was with Bella in the bedroom, preparing to go the convention, while Brooke was on the phone in the other room.

"You okay?" He stepped to Bella and set a hand on her shoulder as they prepared to head over to the convention.

She cupped his hand, sandwiching his between her palm and shoulder, and the gesture warmed some of the chill from his soul. "I'll live." Remorse deepened her tone. "I'm sorry, Matteo. I'm a good shot. But I could've — "

"Don't." He set a finger on her mouth to silence her and smiled. "You were doing your job, and what you had to do. So was I."

"I know you were. And it's okay. I'm not mad at you." Her gaze softened and she lifted her hand to touch his face. "I couldn't stand it if I'd hurt you."

His heart kicked his ribs as he saw deep emotion in her eyes. Saw how much he meant to her.

"You deserve someone better. Someone not so jaded."

"I love your jade eyes." He smiled, trying to lighten her mood. "And it's okay. I'm tough. And damn lucky you've given me, given us, a chance."

"Matteo—"

"Shh. It's okay," he repeated, kissing her nose, refusing to let her even entertain thoughts of walking away. "I love you, Bella." He cupped her face, making sure she held his gaze. "And I told you I'm never leaving you."

She shook as tears shimmered in her eyes. "I'm too lost to be saved, Matteo. I've done things..."

The pain weighing down her words crushed through his chest.

"So have I. You're not alone. Lean on me. Let me be your salvation. Let me be your hero. Let me in, baby. Just let me in." He kissed away the tears spilling down her face and slowly made his way to her trembling lips, determined to show her how he felt, to back up his words.

By the time he drew back, she was clutching him tightly, like she was never going to let him go, and God, that's all he wanted.

"I don't deserve you," she whispered near his ear. "But you're very convincing. And I've been in love with you since I understood the meaning of the word."

He drew back. "Say that again." His chest expanded to accommodate his swelling heart.

"I've been in love with you, and I love you, Matteo. Only you." She kissed him then, long, and deep, and full of the emotions to match the words she'd just spoken.

The sound of a throat clearing registered in his ears.

Reluctantly, he let Bella draw back, and they both turned to look at Brooke smiling in the bedroom doorway.

"Hate to interrupt, but your costumes are here."

He met Bella's gaze. "Let's go find that gas." She nodded. "It'showtime."

***

Two hours later, Bella was still reeling over the fact the sanctioning to kill Rasheed had been rescinded. But she understood the reasoning. Her only hope was that someday that ruling would be lifted. She took a little solace in the fact she'd made the bastard bleed.

Too bad he'd been unconscious at the time.

And her stomach still hollowed out as the scene with Rasheed played out in her head. She'd been confident in her shooting skills at the time, but now…as the scene replayed over and over in her head…God, she could've hit Matteo.

"I'm fine," he said, squeezing her hand, reassuring her for probably the sixth time since the shooting.

She turned to face him, and couldn't help it, she laughed. Hard not to when he had a green mask on his face and Santa hat on his head. Nearly the exact replica of the mask and hat she wore. "You're also green."

"And hot under this stupid thing." He pulled her aside, into a room full of green masked people laughing and dancing and drinking with care through their masks. "But if we don't find that canister soon, we'll be white."

Because they'd be dead. "Roger. Any updates?"

"The kitchen is clear. Vents have been checked and rechecked. And the bathrooms have all been searched."

"That leaves this room," she said. "Rasheed singing yet?"

He shook his head. "Knight's still on it. If anyone can get him to talk, Knight can."

True. But she was less than hopeful he'd succeed.

She already knew how it'd play out. One of the agencies would step in, and Rasheed would head to prison, with the probability of some more of his followers breaking him free again.

Her stomach soured at the thought of that man free to put innocent lives at risk like the ones in this hotel casino. She stiffened.

"What is it?" Matteo asked.

"What if we're looking in the wrong place?" she asked.

He straightened his spine. "I'm listening."

"Is a couple of hundred people dressed in green a big enough target? Or a couple of thousand guests at this hotel?"

"Shit. You're right." He stepped close. "You work here. Where would the biggest impact be?"

"Casino floor," she answered without hesitation. "And, Matteo…" she grabbed his arm. "They pump oxygen into the air."

"Fuck. That's it." He pulled out his phone and made a call.

Bella pulled out her phone too. "Brooke, get TJ to kill the air at the Capris. Now."

"Where?" Brooke asked.

"All of it."

"Roger. Out."

Matteo ended his call and grabbed her hand "Come on. Homeland's on their way to the electrical room. Let's go help." He tugged her through the room and the door where they bumped into a few stragglers in the hall. "Sorry," Matteo said.

Two of them smiled and told them no problem, while a third muttered and oath in French.

She recognized the miserable French Canadian from one of the shops several doors down from Santarelli's. A shop she avoided. They were unfriendly and way overpriced. They took two steps when Matteo suddenly stopped and turned back around.

"What?" It was her turn to question his "aha" moment.

But he was frowning at the French Canadian. "Hey. Wait!" he called to the man still loitering in the area outside the ballroom, as if waiting for someone. Or something. The hall also happened to be only a short distance from the casino floor. "Tremblay."

The man stiffened a second before he took off.

"Get to the electrical room." Matteo gripped her by the upper arms. "Save the innocent like your dad did in New York." Then he released her and charged after the guy.

Bella hesitated all of one second. The choice was a no brainer. She raced after Matteo. Homeland could handle the search for the gas. Be the heroes. Matteo was on his own. Even though he was more than capable of handling things himself, he needed backup.

It hit her as she had his six, that this was the same situation she'd been in with the Russians. No wonder he'd had such a strong reaction. The pressure gripping her chest and was crushing. She longed to pull out her Sig and kneecap the sucker, but there were too many innocents who could get caught in the crossfire. No doubt the same reason Matteo continued to pursue instead of shoot.

The fact Tremblay avoided the casino floor only added to that gripping pressure in her chest. Bastard was definitely Rasheed's secret partner. She hoped to God Homeland found that canister in time.

He was also a pussy. Didn't even stop to take a stand and fight.

Of course, if she had a two-hundred-pound muscled Grinch-Reaper SEAL barreling after her, she'd...well, the point was moot. She'd never be a Tremblay. Never help terrorists. She stopped them. Like her dad.

So did Matteo.

As Tremblay neared the exit to the boardwalk, Matteo dove through the air and tackled the bastard to the ground, crashing into a wall. Screams echoed around the entrance, and people began to run in all directions.

"Gun!" someone shouted, and her heart hit her feet that weren't running fast enough.

Dammit.

As if in slow motion, she watched in horror as Tremblay pulled a gun from under his suit coat while Matteo held the guy pinned to the floor by his throat.

Screw it. She reached into the boot of her costume and yanked out her Sig, deciding to take her chances with the innocent since they'd cleared the area.

"Tremblay," she yelled, taking aim.

The man flicked his gaze to her, and in that split-second, Matteo grabbed Tremblay's gun just before it went off.

"Matteo." She rushed the final twenty feet, unable to breathe, until Matteo rose to his feet. Unharmed.

Tremblay did not.

As several agents came running onto the scene and took over, she holstered her gun and barreled into Matteo.

"It's okay," he said, yanking their masks off before wisely holding her tight, because, damn, all the strength seemed to drain from her legs. "I'm okay." His lips brushed her temple. "Are you lost? Pretty sure access to the electrical room is in the back of the casino."

She chuckled, then drew back and punched his shoulder. Hard. "Don't scare me like that."

He chuckled now, too. "Ouch. Hey. It was either him or me."

She stilled and blinked at him, more than a little turned on by the fact he'd used her words against her. "Yeah, well, let's finish this up, because it's going to be me and you, and a lot of adrenaline to work off soon. Hope you have some ideas on how we can go about that."

His gaze smoldered as he smiled into her face. "Oh. I've got plenty. I'll take care of you. You just had my six. It's only fair that I return the favor."

***

Matteo was only half listening to the Homeland agent who was explaining how the canister of gas was found attached to the casino ventilation system housed in the electrical room, and was missed the first time because the system for the ballroom was in a different location. All bull. To him, someone dropped the ball. If one ventilation system needed to be checked, they all needed to be checked.

End of story.

He glanced over at Bella, who was talking with Brooke and a few FBI agents who'd arrived from D.C. She looked absolutely adorable wearing a backpack over half of a sexy Grinch outfit, minus the mask and hat. He was looking forward to minusing the outfit from her too.

"Excuse me," he said, interrupting the agent, to point to his woman. "I'm needed over there."

And the fact it was true made his steps lighter, as he headed to Bella. He needed her too. And he intended to show her just how much, if he could ever get her alone. They'd been at this for hours.

"Hi." She smiled up at him, with her whole heart reflected in her gaze, and God, it was the most amazing gift she could ever give him.

"Hello, beautiful." He slid his arm around her shoulders and tugged her against him, vaguely aware of the FBI dudes excusing themselves, then he turned his attention to Brooke. "Any word from Knight? Are we good to go?"

The woman smiled. "I believe things are wrapping up here. But I haven't heard from him yet."

He nodded.

"What's wrong?" Bella frowned up at him.

Something niggled at his brain. Had been for the past few hours. He'd hoped once the gas canister was found and safely removed that the niggling would cease.

It didn't.

He lifted a shoulder. "Not sure."

If one system needed to be checked, they all needed to be checked.

His earlier thought resounded in his head again. "Tremblay."

"What about him?" Bella narrowed her gaze. "He's dead."

"His sister. Anyone have eyes on her?" He never got a good read from those two.

Brooke's phone rang. "It's Knight," she told them before answering. "I was just about to call you, sir." The woman straightened her spine. "Interesting. Yes, sir. I'll tell them."

"Tremblay doesn't have a sister."

"What?" He reeled back.

Bella stiffened. "Then who was the woman?"

"A radical for the cause. The two of them were posing as brother and sister. Simpson brought them in, set up their shop for them to establish their cover while they awaited their instructions."

"That explained why their merchandise was overpriced." He shook his head. "They had no idea how to run a business."

Bella released him and straightened her spine. "Where is she? We need to find her. This convention was just the test. She's going to carry out the bigger target."

Son-of-a-bitch.

"It's okay. Knight caught up with her and Simpson, heading to New York City with a half dozen canisters in their trunk."

He let out a breath and so did Bella.

"Thank God," she said. "I know it's Knight and all, but how the hell did he know?"

Matteo was wondering the same damn thing.

Brooke smiled at them. "Paresh."

Bella sucked in a breath and seemed to hold it.

He slid an arm around her shoulders as he continued to question Brooke. "What happened?"

"He told his dad last night about the mess he was in, and his father contacted a lawyer. Then the lawyer contacted Homeland."

His back straightened. "So was he with them today when Homeland was rounding up Kamal and Tariq?"

"Yes." Brooke nodded.

Bella slumped back against. "Okay. I think I've had enough excitement for one day."

"True." He chuckled. "Today was a two-day kind of excitement day."

She snorted. "Yeah. Well, I think I'm good until next year."

Laughing, Matteo turned her to face him. "Next year is a week away."

"A week, huh?" She bit her lower lip, and a wicked gleam entering her eyes. "Whatever can we do to substitute for the guns and canister bomb kind of excitement?"

"Don't worry." He winked. "I've got your six."

Epilogue

Not quite an hour into the new year, Bella fell back onto the mattress, dragging in air next to an equally spent Matteo.

"Damn, frogman," she said after catching her breath. "We're going to kill each other."

A chuckle rumbled in his throat. He turned onto his side and traced her lower lip with his finger. "You're crazy, you know that?"

"You're just realizing that now?"

He slid his hand to cup her cheek and neck, the movement turning her face toward his, and her breath caught at the emotions visible in his open gaze. "I've always known, baby. It's one of the reasons why I love you so much."

She lifted her hand to hold his face. "I love you, too, Matteo. So much."

One thing she'd learned over the past decade was that falling in love with him was a blessing and a curse.

And she was happy to have come full circle with him.

"It's a brand new year," she said, excited by the possibilities.

"Yep." He smiled. "Dad will be home soon, and he's chomping at the bit to get back to work. Thank God, because I'm done tossing dough."

Luckily, his father had made a ninety-percent recovery. He'd need some speech therapy for a while, but that was minor compared to the alternative.

She traced a line from his shoulder to his bicep with her finger. "Yeah, you're more suited to be a Knight than a pizzaiolo."

He dipped down to nip at her chin. "You going to be happy as a Knight?"

"Absolutely. Someone taught me the merits of having one's six." She'd handed in her resignation last week. No more leaving him. Where he went, she went. As it turned out, they were going to work from their hometown.

Knight asked them to head a northeastern satellite office for the Knight Agency, right here in Atlantic City.

"Or front." He ran his palm lightly down her body, brushing over her nipple on the way to her belly. Her whole body quivered to life. He chuckled.

Damn him.

How could he know what she wanted before she did? Give what she needed before she demanded? Take what she wanted to give him?

Matteo's gaze met hers and held as he slowly lowered his mouth.

But he didn't kiss her immediately. He hovered, breath warming her face, amping up the anticipation, making her pulse race out of control.

God, she loved this man.

She lifted her face to meet him halfway and he pressed her down into the mattress. There was nothing like being underneath Matteo's hot body. Bella slid her hands around his neck and wrapped her leg around his, ripping a deliciously sexy growl deep in his throat.

He broke the kiss and smiled down at her. "

"You know, I never did ask Knight if it was forbidden to fraternize with a coworker." She glided her palm down his side. "Think it'll be a problem?"

Heat smoldered in his gaze as his lips brushed her cheek on the way to her mouth. "Nothing is forbidden anymore."

***

If you enjoyed GRINCH REAPER, *please consider leaving a review. Thank you.*

*The danger all started in Lisa's story, **Knight's SEAL**, and continues in Nikki's story **LOCKE and Load**, Gina's story, **A Daye with a SEAL**, Tarah's story, **Cowboy LAWE**,* a connection to Kat's story in, **Elite Protector**, and a connection to Isabelle's story in, Grinch Reaper, with more stories, connected stories and crossovers to come in the ***Dangerous Curves Series**!*

Visit DonnaMichaelsAuthor.com sign up for her Newsletter. Enjoy exclusive reads, enter subscriber only contests, and be the first to know about upcoming books!

***

Find out who the Commander calls next. Make sure to pick up ALL the books in the Sleeper SEALs Series. These can be read in any order and each stands alone.

Protecting Dakota by Susan Stoker

Slow Ride by Becky McGraw

Michael's Mercy by Dale Myer

Saving Zola by Becca Jameson

Bachelor SEAL by Sharon Hamilton

Montana Rescue by Elle James

Thin Ice by Maryann Jordan

Grinch Reaper by Donna Michaels

All In by Lori Ryan

Broken SEAL by Geri Foster

Freedom Code by Elaine Levine

Flat Line by J.M. Madden

Visit DonnaMichaelsAuthor.com and sign up for her Newsletter. Enjoy exclusive reads, enter subscriber only contests, and be the first to know about upcoming books!

♥

ALSO BY DONNA MICHAELS
Amazon.com/author.donna-michaels

~*Dangerous Curves Series*~
Knight's SEAL –KW (#1)
Locke and Load (#2)
A DAYE with a SEAL–KW (#3)
Cowboy LAWE (#4)

~*Citizen Soldier Novels*~
(Harland County Spinoff Series)
Wyne and Dine (#1) (Award Winning)
Wyne and Chocolate (#2)
Wyne and Song (#3)
Wine and Her New Year Cowboy (#4)
Whine and Rescue KW(#5)
Wine and Hot Shoes (#6)
Wine and Scenery (#7)

~*Harland County Series*~
Harland County Christmas (Prequel)
Her Fated Cowboy (#1)
Her Unbridled Cowboy (#2)
Her Uniform Cowboy (#3) (Award Winning)
Her Forever Cowboy (#4) (Award Winning)
Her Healing Cowboy (#5)
Her Volunteer Cowboy (#6)
Her Indulgent Cowboy (#7)
Her Hell Yeah Cowboy (#8) (Sable Hunter's Hell
Yeah! KW Crossover Novella)

Her Troubled Cowboy (#9) (Citizen Soldier Crossover)
Her Hell No Cowboy (#10) (Sable Hunter's Hell Yeah! KW Crossover Novella)

~The Men of At Ease Ranch Series~
~Entangled Publications~
In An Army Ranger's Arms (#1)
Her Secret Army Ranger (#2)
The Right Army Ranger (#3)
Army Ranger with Benefits (#4) rel. 03/12/18

~Time-shift Heroes Series~
Captive Hero (#1)
Future Cowboy Hero (#2) (tba)

~Related~
Cowboy-Fiancé (formerly Cowboy-Sexy) (*Hand drawn Japanese Translation*)
Cowboy Payback (sequel)

~Novels~
She Does Know Jack
Royally Unleashed
The Spy Who Fanged Me

~Novellas~
Thanks for Giving
Ten Things I'd Do for a Cowboy
Vampire Kristmas

DonnaMichaelsAuthor.com

Connect with Donna Online

Donna's Facebook Profile:
https://www.facebook.com/DonnaMichaelsAuthor

Follow Donna on Twitter:
https://twitter.com/Donna_Michaels

Find Donna's Books on Goodreads:
http://www.goodreads.com/Donna_Michaels

Email: Donna_Michaels@msn.com

Website: www.DonnaMichaelsAuthor.com

To sign up for Donna's Newsletter go to:

http://tinyurl.com/zaxbqe6

Amazon:
http://www.amazon.com/Donna-Michaels/e/B008J24XR2/

Bookbub:
https://www.bookbub.com/authors/donna-michaels

About the Author

Donna Michaels Donna Michaels is an award winning, *New York Times & USA Today* bestselling author of *Romaginative* fiction. Her hot, humorous, and heartwarming stories include cowboys, men in uniform, and some sexy primal alphas who are equally matched by their heroines. With a husband recently retired from the military, a household of six, and several rescued cats, she never runs out of material. From short to epic, her books entertain readers across a variety of sub-genres, one was even hand-drawn into a Japanese translation. Published through Entangled Publications, The Wild Rose Press, Whimsical Publications, and self-published, she entertains readers across a variety of sub-genres, and one book is even being hand drawn into a Japanese translation....if only she could read it...

Bringing you HEAs-One Hot Alpha Hero at a Time

Thanks for reading,
~Donna

Up next Sleeper SEAL sneak peek

Turn the page to get a sneak peek at

Lori Ryan's ALL IN

Chapter One

"Have you heard from Naomi?"

Luke Reynolds looked at his brother as they crossed the road to the sandwich shop. They didn't have a lot of time for lunch since Zach was on the job, but they needed to talk. "Yeah. I talked to her a couple of days ago. She's still not thrilled with either of us."

Zach had the decency to look chagrined. "We probably went a little overboard," he finally said, as he held the door open for Luke.

Luke ordered their usual sandwiches while Zach grabbed them two bottles of iced tea apiece and a family-sized bag of chips for them to split.

Luke answered as he paid the cashier and the two moved down the counter to wait for their lunch. "Yeah." He scrubbed at the bristle covering his jaw. He needed to shave. "Maybe. I don't know."

He replayed the scene from a week back in his head. As soon as he'd seen the way those college assholes had looked at Naomi, he'd known they should have insisted she attend an all-girls school. Or stayed home and attended school locally. Or stayed locked in her room forever.

He looked at Zach. "We've been that age. You know as well as I do what those assholes were thinking as soon as they saw her. Hell, they were practically lined up along the sidewalks watching for fresh meat, and drooling while they did it. It didn't hurt anything for them to know she's got some muscle at home ready to defend her."

Zach hadn't raised Naomi the way Luke had, but he was almost as defensive of her. Sadly, raising his niece from the age of ten had taught Luke his gut instinct where she was concerned wasn't usually the right one. He'd gotten a lot of things wrong where she was concerned. She was usually more patient with him than any parent had a right to expect. But judging by the look on her face when she'd heard Zach and Luke growling at the male students when they'd dropped her off for her freshman year of school at Dartmouth College, he probably should have curbed his gut instincts.

He hadn't.

"But she's okay, otherwise?" Zach asked, grabbing the bag offered by the woman behind the deli counter with a nod. They walked outdoors and sat at one of the few small tables lining the sidewalk outside the deli, taking a few minutes to open their food and dig in.

"Yeah." Luke spoke around a large bite of turkey and cheese on whole grain bread. "Says she got into the classes she wanted and she likes her roommate so far. How's Shauna?"

Shauna and Zach had been dating for several months and Luke had to admit, he liked her for Zach. She was strong and sharp and just what his brother needed.

The goofy look on Zach's face could have answered for him. "She's good."

"She move in yet?" It seemed the next logical step for the pair, but Luke wasn't sure if Zach realized just how far gone he was for the woman.

Zach shrugged. "Soon. So, you gonna make it a habit to show up here for lunches?" He leveled Luke with a look. It wasn't every day that Luke showed up at the New Haven Police Department where Zach was a detective to drag him out for lunch.

Luke shrugged.

"You know you're like a housewife suffering from that empty nest shit, right? I mean you get how pitiful you are, right?"

Luke bounced a pickle off Zach's forehead, but it only earned him a laugh from his brother. He wasn't going to tell Zach he'd caught himself singing *House at Pooh Corner* the other day. That had been Naomi's bedtime song when she was younger.

Hell, he still sang it to her on occasion, but it was better Zach not know that he'd started singing it to himself since she moved out. That would give Zach fodder for taunting him for decades.

Zach was right about one thing, though. Luke didn't have a clue what to do with his life now that Naomi wasn't at home. Now that she didn't need him the same way she had.

Leaving the SEAL teams hadn't been easy for Luke, but it had been the right move for Naomi, who'd lost everything in one split second of stupidity.

Luke saw Zach's movements slow until his brother was staring at him, no longer eating.

Zach's voice was low when he spoke. "What's up?"

Luke chugged his first iced tea before opening his second. "I might be out-of-pocket for a little while. Just didn't want you to worry if I'm not around much." He and his brother had gotten used to seeing each other often since Zach made it a point to visit Naomi at least once a week, if not more. With the job he'd just taken on, that wouldn't be as likely. Luke would be keeping a low profile, and stopping by the precinct to see his detective brother wouldn't really fit with his assignment.

Zach tried to play the moment off as a joke. "I know you're not heading back to the teams. You're too damned old for that shit."

Luke grinned, giving Zach the levity he'd been looking for. "I can still swim circles around your tired ass, little brother." They both knew as a former SEAL, Luke could beat Zach in anything having to do with water.

They continued eating in silence for several minutes before Zach spoke again. "Anything you can tell me about?"

He had to know the answer, but Luke gave it to him anyway. "No."

"You got anyone watching your back?"

Luke shook his head, no, and rolled up the paper his sandwich had come in, ignoring the curse from Zach.

Zach looked around. There were plenty of people walking by their table, but none were paying attention to their conversation. "So, you're pulling a one-eighty? Going from safe and sound and no risk to throwing yourself into . . . into what?"

Luke didn't answer. Since their mother, sister, and brother-in-law had died in a car accident that stole everything from Naomi, Luke had taken the safest path he could find in life. He'd chosen to work running background checks instead of accepting any number of offers to do private security work or attend the police academy the way Zach had after his own separation from the military.

Zach continued. "She went off to college, but she still needs you. She still needs to know you're not putting yourself in the line of fire."

"Says the man who came home from the military to work as a cop." Luke couldn't help but feel some resentment. He'd never in a million years go back and change what he did when his sister and mom died. He'd never regret taking Naomi. Family was family, and you gave everything to family.

But that didn't change the fact that Zach had been able to do things Luke had felt he couldn't do. Zach hadn't played things safe the way Luke had. He'd been there for Naomi, same as Luke, but not in the quite the same way. He wasn't the one Naomi woke up to when she had a nightmare or relied on when she was sick or scared. Zach hadn't taken on being mother and father, as well as uncle.

"Look, Naomi will always be my top priority. Always. That doesn't mean I can keep sitting at home while she's . . . " He let that die out. If he finished the sentence with *while she's off living life* like he wanted to, he'd sound like a royal wuss. But it was the truth. She was starting to build her own life independent of him.

Zach had his own life. He had a career. He had purpose.

Luke had a business, but it was a business he'd been doing as a placeholder and it had always felt that way to him. He'd been running online background checks for people. Things couldn't get any safer—or more boring—than that.

He wasn't going to run off to fight a war, but the job he'd been tapped for wasn't one he could turn his back on. Too much was at stake for that.

Zach must have read the look on Luke's. Luke wasn't willing to discuss the issue further. Zach sighed. "Just know I've got your back if you need me. You might think you're working this one on your own, but that won't ever be the case, you got me?"

Luke grunted and tossed another pickle, hitting Zach square between the eyes and earning a grin.

Chapter Two

Lyra Hill hugged her brother as they stood on the front steps of her apartment building. With her on the step above him, they were almost the same height. "You're a lifesaver."

He shrugged but the accompanying grin was cocky. "Eh, no biggie. I love hanging with my girls." He turned to the four-year-old twins currently hawking the front door of the building waiting for someone to open the heavy glass and let them in.

When her boss had called her in on a day she should have been working at home, her brother had saved her by taking Alyssa and Prentiss for the day. They were likely sugared up, but she'd been able to get to the office for a few hours. According to the rundown Alyssa had given Lyra at warp speed upon their return, they'd convinced him to take them to the park followed by a trip for ice cream. Not just ice cream in a cup or a cone the way she would have. Real ice cream sundaes with double cherries and hot fudge. And, as Prentiss had put it with her nose all crinkled in the look she usually reserved for spinach, "no nuts."

The girls got their wish for the umpteenth time that day when Mrs. Lawson from 1C came out and held the door for the girls so they could scoot in ahead of Lyra.

Lyra rolled her eyes at Billy as the girls raced into the building and around the corner out of sight. She normally had a rule they had to stay in her line of vison, but they knew that rule wasn't applied very stringently in the apartment building. The neighbors kept an eye out on the girls.

"I better catch up to them." She waved as he walked away and turned to follow the twins.

Mrs. Lawson fanned her face. "Prepare yourself, honey. Hot and steamy hunk in there. I think he might have melted my glasses."

Lyra's feet slowed. "Huh?"

"You'll see." Mrs. Lawson gave Lyra a look as she continued to fan herself. "I've always hoped maybe you and my Murphy would get together, but even I have to admit he can't compete with *this*."

Mrs. Lawson walked away before Lyra could formulate an answer. She was a little stuck on the idea of her and Mrs. Lawson's grandson, Murphy, together. Mrs. Lawson had never mentioned that, and Lyra could honestly say she'd never once gone there in her own head. Not that there was anything wrong with Mrs. Lawson's grandson. He was just so . . . well, so . . . nice. And tame. And, well, boring, if Lyra really thought about it.

Not to mention, he hadn't once seemed interested in her. In fact, she thought he might be gay, but they'd never talked enough for her to know for sure.

"Huh," Lyra said, again, this time a statement instead of a question and very much to herself as she followed the girls inside since Mrs. Lawson hadn't bothered to stick around long enough to explain anything.

Holy Mary Mother of . . . The thought plain petered out in Lyra's head as her brain melted. At least only Mrs. Lawson' glasses had fallen victim. For Lyra, it seemed her whole damned head had suffered the damage.

The man in front of her was not tame in the least. He was nothing short of a god. The kind of chiseled jaw you read about, dark brown hair that somehow screamed for a girl to paw at it, and five o'clock shadow to die for. That was to say nothing of his body. He was currently kneeling before her girls.

"Are you a real superhero?" Alyssa was asking. Lyra had noticed the shirt the man was wearing as well, though likely not for the same reasons her daughter had.

Lyra was looking at the way it pulled taught over broad muscled shoulders and a chest that made her breath catch. Alyssa was likely referring to the Captain America logo on the front of it.

The man raised soul-searing eyes and winked at Lyra before lowering his voice to answer Alyssa with a conspirator's whisper. "I'm not supposed to give away my secret identity. That's lesson number one of being a good superhero." He assumed a more bashful look. "Honestly, though, I'm still working on my superhero identity. I'm a little new at it and I haven't ironed out all the kinks."

Kink. Lyra shook her head at her reaction to the man. This was *not* at all like her. Then again, it wasn't like she dated a whole lot. Being a single mom of four-year-old twins could take a toll on a girl's social life. She stepped closer and put her hand on Alyssa's shoulder. Not that it would slow down her little girl's questions. Alyssa wasn't shy about going after what she wanted, and answers were no exception. Prentiss, on the other hand, was happy to stand silently by and listen as Alyssa did all the work.

Lyra couldn't help but notice she was listening avidly, though. She was as interested in the answers as Alyssa was.

"Can you introduce us to Wonder Woman?"

The man let out a big laugh at Alyssa's question and tugged at one of the twisty pigtails framing her face. "Sorry. Like I said, I'm new at this. I have no clout with Wonder Woman yet. She's a little high up in the ranks, you know?"

He stood to his full height and thrust a hand toward Lyra. "I'm Luke Reynolds. I'll be your super for the next month."

Lyra took his hand and mentally swatted at the swoon happening in her head as his warm hand engulfed hers. She could practically hear her girlfriends giggling and telling her to enjoy the moment.

She shook the voices right out of her head and smiled. "What happened to Kyle?" Kyle was the young doctorate student who normally served, for better or worse, as the building's super.

Alyssa answered for him, so they must have already covered this territory. Leave it to Alyssa to challenge anyone new in the building. "He's counting testicles."

Lyra could feel the heat race to her face as her eyes shot to the man in front of her, but her new super took it in stride. He looked down at Alyssa, the edges of his lips twitching as a smile tried to break free. "Tentacles. He's counting tentacles." Now he turned to Lyra. "Kyle is going to be on board a marine biology vessel tracking a mutation in the number of legs in some kind of octopus for the next month. From what I'm told, it's a dream internship for someone in his field."

"Ah." Lyra nodded.

Kyle was a nice enough kid, but he wasn't the greatest super in the world. He tried, but his skill level at fixing things left something to be desired. She could put up with looking at this guy for the next month for sure, and who knew, maybe he'd turn out to be good at fixing things as a bonus.

Her friends' voices were back in her head with all kinds of comments about fixing things, complete with Joey Tribbiani-style grins and nods.

"Anyway, you're stuck with me." Luke smiled again and damn if her panties didn't start trying to wriggle right off. This had to end. Had to.

Prentiss tugged on her sleeve, drawing Lyra's attention back to the girls.

"Uncle Billy says I can take apart his old clock." Prentiss pulled a digital alarm clock from her backpack and looked up at Lyra patiently, wide brown eyes waiting.

"Oh goodie." Lyra pulled her keys from her bag and moved toward their door, marked 1B. "Sorry," she said over her shoulder to her new across-the-hall neighbor and temporary eye candy, "apparently, we've got technology to reverse engineer."

Alyssa rolled her eyes. Unlike her twin, she was much more into fashion than engineering. "I have to plan our outfits for tomorrow." She said this to Luke as though he should understand it, and he nodded with equal solemnity, not missing a beat.

Lyra wondered if he had kids.

"Hey, let me know if you come up with any ideas on that superhero identity thing. I can use all the help I can get." His expression was completely serious and Lyra was now sure he must have kids, or maybe nieces and nephews at the very least. Some small part of her hoped it was nieces and nephews and not a wife and kids.

It sucked when he caught her looking for a ring on his finger a heartbeat later. She blushed and turned away. "Okay, girls, let's get out of Luke's hair."

And get him out of mommy's head. She must be tired. The man was criminally good looking, but still, he shouldn't be such a distraction. She had dinner to prep and lunch boxes to wash and reload for the morning. She didn't have time to fantasize about things like the Incredible Hunk or Handsome Man or any number of just-right superhero names she could come up with for her new neighbor.

Grab Lori Ryan's ALL IN at all major retailers

31978338R00149

Printed in Great Britain
by Amazon